Errol Lloyd

Many Rivers to Cross

mammoth

To Joan-ann, Asana and Mica who abided with me while this book was being written; to all those friends, too numerous to mention by name, who shared with me some meaningful snippet of their lives to help enliven these pages; to my editor Miriam Hodgson, who gently coaxed this book out of me, and finally to all those who made the crossing.

First published in Great Britain 1995
by Methuen Children's Books Ltd
Published 1996 by Mammoth
an imprint of Egmont Children's Books Limited
239 Kensington High Street, London W8 6SA

Reprinted 1997, 1998, 1999 (twice)

Copyright © 1995 Errol Lloyd

The moral rights of the author and cover illustrator
have been asserted.

ISBN 0 7497 2589 3

A CIP catalogue record for this book is available from the British Library

Printed and bound in Great Britain by Cox & Wyman Ltd, Reading, Berkshire

Contents

Part One – Jamaica, 1966

1	The Letter	3
2	Unexpected News	11
3	The Passport Photo	16
4	'My granddaughter going to England'	22
5	Farewells	26
6	Moonlight	34
7	Granny's Grace	36

Part Two – Crossing Over

8	Annette	45
9	'You have sapadillas?'	49
10	The Storm	54

Part Three – England

11	The Meeting	63
12	Home	70
13	'When is Leroy coming up, Mamma?'	75
14	'She's not my sister'	79
15	Off to School	84
16	Alone	90

17 'My thoughts are with you'   97

18 Christmas   106

19 The Test   116

20 'I wish you left me in Jamaica . . .'   120

21 'I am beginning to like England'   127

22 Moving House   133

23 Carnival   141

24 Last Leaves of Autumn   146

25 Flowers for Granny   150

PART ONE – JAMAICA, 1966

1 The Letter

The first thing that came to Sandra's mind when she awoke was the letter.

She was sure it wasn't a figment of her imagination that yesterday, just as she had entered Granny's room, she had seen her hurriedly hide a letter in her bedside drawer. What was more, she was sure that it was a letter from her mother in England.

She had said nothing but waited patiently for Granny to choose her own time to read it to her and Leroy, her brother. Granny usually read letters after supper when they were sitting on the veranda with nothing in particular to do and Granny would entertain them with all kinds of stories: Brer Anancy stories, 'duppy' or ghost stories, or just family stories. But a letter from England always came first.

But last night no letter was read, and what's more Granny seemed to be pretending that none existed. Why all the secrecy? wondered Sandra.

'Wake up, chile, or we'll be late for church,' shouted Granny, interrupting her thoughts.

Sandra didn't want to go to church and rolled over.

'Too much bed mek head dull,' continued Granny.

There was no letting-up with Granny, Sandra thought. She rubbed the sleep from her eyes and walked, zombie-like, to the cistern to wash. She cleaned her teeth with a chew stick dipped in a mixture of ash and salt. She smiled as it was so typical of Granny to make them use these. Granny had stoutly resisted buying toothbrushes and toothpaste. They only rotted your teeth, she said, and teeth could only be kept healthy and white if cleaned in the traditional way.

Sandra took off the large T-shirt that acted as a nighty and, in one swift action lest her courage failed her, she opened the tap and darted under the cold water that streamed from the bare pipe jutting out from the wall. Her teeth chattered as the water noisily bounced off her body on to the concrete floor before gurgling away down a hole.

With the towel wrapped round her, she made her way back to the bedroom and hurriedly dried herself. She reached for the new white bra, which she was putting on for the first time.

Granny was shocked when Sandra had asked her to buy her one.

'What you want brassière for, girl?' she had demanded.

Sandra hadn't answered, but stood facing her, allowing her to survey the evidence in front of her eyes.

'Good Lord, chile, you turning a big woman on me for true!' she shrieked.

Sandra smiled at Granny's exaggerated response. Leroy, two years older than her, had borne the brunt of this standard adult reaction in recent years. 'What a way you turn a big man!' friends and relatives alike would say. 'They grow up so quick these days, eh?' or 'Time really fly for true, nuh?'

'Look at that, eh!' continued Granny when she had recovered from the shock. 'Just yesterday you was a little gal pickney hanging on to your mother coat tail.'

In the end Granny promised her a 'brassière', but it had taken her three weeks to get around to it, as if she wasn't yet fully convinced that her little twelve-year-old granddaughter was growing up.

Still in front of the mirror, Sandra shifted her torso from angle to angle like a model, trying to appraise the bra and its effect. She felt a surge of pride. But it was pride tinged with fear of a kind that was new to her and to which she couldn't put a name.

'Hurry and get yourself ready, chile,' reproached Granny as she passed the half-open door that connected their rooms. 'And move from in front of that mirror.'

'Granny say you must move from in front the mirror!' echoed

Leroy from his bedroom before the words were properly out of Granny's mouth.

'Give me a chance, nuh!' retorted Sandra.

'Leroy, don't wind up you sister, you hear!'

'She already wind herself up, Granny.'

'I don't want no backchat. Just hurry and get dressed, both of you!'

'Granny say to hurry and get dressed,' said Leroy, pushing his luck.

'Shut up, Leroy!' hissed Sandra.

'Lord, if you see my dying trial,' moaned Granny, with eyes uplifted to the heavens in supplication. 'Children! I too old for all this now!'

Sandra could never figure out what a 'dying trial' was. It was Granny's favourite expression when overcome with anger or frustration. Fortunately, in spite of Granny's numerous 'dying trials', she was still alive and kicking.

Sandra pulled on her new frilly frock, feeling a bit cross that she had no time to admire it. She then slipped on her new high-heel shoes, her *pièce de résistance*. Her eyes seemed glued to the new shoes as she walked tentatively towards the kitchen where Granny had poured mugs of steaming tea.

'Where is that brother of yours?' Granny demanded and, without waiting for an answer, shouted, 'Leroy, your tea ready.'

It wasn't the kind of tea sold in fancy boxes in the village grocery store that the better-off people bought. It was one of Granny's own 'bush' teas, made from the freshly picked leaves of plants that she cultivated all around the yard. Today it was fever-grass tea, which was yellowy green and drunk with a little sugar to take away the bitterness. A mug of tea was all they were ever allowed before church, because Granny didn't believe that the Lord approved of those who worshipped on a full stomach. There would be enough time for all that indulgence after church.

After a few hurried gulps of her tea, Sandra dashed through the front door clutching her handbag, trying to catch up with Granny and Leroy who were already walking briskly towards the church.

'Hurry up, girl,' said Granny with hardly a backward glance.

5

'You don't hear what Granny say!' said Leroy, rubbing salt in the wound, for he saw the trouble she had walking in her new shoes.

'Mind your own business, Leroy!' retorted Sandra sticking out her tongue at him in mock anger: she knew she must look funny. The heels were barely a couple of inches off the ground but Sandra had wanted a pair with even higher heels.

'Please, please, Granny, Jennifer Allen wear high heels, and she's only eleven!' pleaded Sandra.

'I don't care how old she is!'

'And she has really high heels . . .'

'If you can't get turkey, you must satisfy with John Crow,' retorted Granny with finality, 'so stop pestering me, Sandra James.'

It was nine o'clock and the sun was already high in the sky. In spite of the gentle sea breeze, beads of perspiration gathered on Granny's brows and ran down the creases in her face like tiny tributaries. Granny always seemed to feel the heat more than Leroy and Sandra. She mopped her brow and her face every now and then with a handkerchief, which she carried in the sleeve of her frock.

Granny had the same high, well-defined James forehead as her two grandchildren. But it was difficult to trace any other resemblance. Granny had a rusty brown, almost reddish complexion, with an aquiline nose and narrow lips which revealed a mixture of European and African ancestry. Both Leroy and Sandra had the cool black complexions and the soft African features of their mother's side of the family.

Sandra had narrow almond-shaped eyes above a friendly rounded nose that sat comfortably on her face and full lips that were always threatening to break out into a smile. Granny always told her that she was lucky to be born with a face that made people want to smile when they looked at her. 'If you can mek people laugh, you will go far in this world,' she never tired of saying, invariably breaking into a spontaneous laugh herself, as if counting herself amongst the specially blessed.

As they walked down the lane, the fronds of coconut trees that rose high up into the clear blue skies, stirred and made a soothing rustle. The murmur of the Caribbean sea was punctuated by a cacophony of bells that rang out from rival churches. A solitary John Crow cruised leisurely through the sky on outstretched wings, as if to announce that all was sweetness and light in the world.

'Hurry up, children!' Granny considered it a mortal sin to be late for church, especially as they lived only ten minutes' walk away. Out of politeness, they exchanged hurried greetings with the villagers they met on the way, whether they knew them or not.

Some of the houses they passed were modest zinc-covered houses like theirs, others large four- or five-bedroom houses with cars parked outside. But they all had their cultivated plots where banana and plantain trees, sugar-cane plants and corn stalks jostled for sunlight.

At last the church came into view. They hurried up the steps behind Granny. However much she hustled and bustled outside the church, she always managed to transform herself into a picture of ladylike calm and dignity the minute she entered the building, as if she had been delivered to the church steps by a chauffeur-driven limousine. She had mastered the art of shuffling down the aisle in a kind of hushed reverence, her rounded hips rolling rhythmically in the struggle to prevent her heels from making noisy contact with the cut stone floor.

Sandra tried her best to imitate Granny, but to her acute embarrassment, the heels of her shoes grated noisily against the floor, and heads turned in her direction. There was no shortage of curiosity on the part of the congregation as to who was wearing what.

Now everybody would know she couldn't walk properly in her new high heels! Leroy, shuffling quietly behind her, stifled a giggle.

They hurriedly took their seats. The women kept cool by fanning themselves with little decorated straw fans. The men considered it effeminate to use fans, so they suffered in silence in their stuffy Sunday-best suits and would probably have kept their hats on as well had it not been considered ill-mannered to do so.

Before they could catch their breath, the first hymn was announced and they were on their feet again. The older members of the congregation, Granny chief amongst them, sang their hearts out as if all the cares and sorrows of the world rested on their shoulders and this was the only chance they had to tell anybody about it.

Sandra often found herself daydreaming and fighting the urge to fidget, especially during the sermon which was always too long for her. Now she remembered the unread letter and memories of her mother and father came flooding in. Whenever they had made weekend visits to Granny, they always went to church on Sundays and sat in the very same pew they now occupied.

But the settled pattern of their lives was shattered when Sandra's father decided to go to England. He was in high spirits on the day when he had returned home from Kingston with his entry permit to England stamped in his passport. He had shown it to friends and neighbours with pride and optimism for it was his passport to the good life.

Sandra hadn't given it much thought at first, but as the time for his departure neared, she had felt closer to him. She knew he planned to be away for a year or two and she wanted to savour every last moment with him before he left. She became his faithful assistant when he was home from work and cultivating his garden patch or feeding the chickens or tethering the goats.

But it was now six years since she had stood by the dockside, and cheerfully waved goodbye to him as he boarded the boat for England. She was sure that he would return with that coveted crock of gold and they would live happily ever after. For didn't everybody say that the streets of England were paved with gold? All you had to do was to bend down and pick it up. Not literally, of course, but people believed that an honest hardworking person could work and save and come back home rich.

But there was no crock of gold and her father did not come back.

Leroy was sent to live with Granny, and Sandra was even more

8

upset at parting with Leroy. Her mother persuaded her that it was for the best, it would have been too difficult for her to look after them both on her own.

Sandra knew that Leroy was the apple of her mother's eye, just as she had been her father's favourite. Sometimes when her mother was cross with her and cut her heart with the sharpness of her tongue, she felt sure that her mother would have preferred it if she had been sent away and not Leroy.

Two years later, her mother prepared to leave for England. Sandra couldn't understand why.

'Things don't always work out the way you expect them to,' her mother explained with the bitterness of aloes in her voice.

'Dadda was supposed to come back long time now,' insisted Sandra.

'Times change and plans rearrange,' her mother said drily.

'Why can't all of us go, Mamma? Me and you and Leroy.'

'Don't be stupid, child. Your father have enough trouble finding the money for one fare, let alone three. You must really think money grow on tree!'

Money, money! She should have known it would have been money; money that made grown-ups argue and fight; money that split up families and cast long shadows across the face of the sun.

Bit by bit Sandra began to understand that her father could not return home empty-handed, a failure.

Her mother's departure was a tearful occasion, for Sandra and Leroy had learnt that ships and foghorns and squalling seagulls meant long and bitter separation, broken families and fractured dreams.

Granny's house, though modest, had three bedrooms which meant that Sandra had a room all to herself. She remembered how she had clung to her doll that night and sobbed until she fell asleep. She was never quite sure if she wept at losing her mother or because she was not going with her to see her long-lost father.

But at least she was reunited with Leroy. When she went to the secondary school, or 'big school' as everybody called it, Leroy was already there to smooth her path.

Within a year she acquired a new brother and sister, for her

9

mother gave birth to twins, Wayne and Jean. Sandra was sad that she couldn't be with them. It wasn't much fun having a long-distance family. All she had to cuddle was a photograph of the twins sitting together in their double push-chair looking like identical peas in a pod with their proud parents beaming in the background. She had to remind herself that they were her parents too.

She was jolted back to the reality of the present by the announcement of the last hymn. The last hymn always seemed the best so Sandra joined in with genuine enthusiasm.

After church, people gathered in little clusters or milled about chatting and exchanging gossip. The preacher positioned himself at the front door and shook everybody's hand as they left the church. He was a jolly man with a round black face and a broad smile.

'Lovely pair of shoes,' he said to Sandra as he squeezed her hand. 'Lovely pair of shoes.'

This Granny took as an invitation to give the preacher chapter and verse of when and where the shoes were purchased, down to the size and the height of the heels.

'Two inches or so is fine for the heel,' offered Granny.

'They all wear high-heel shoes in the end,' said the parson with a smile, as if he was anxious to reassure Granny that it was perfectly acceptable in God's eyes for young girls to grow up.

2 Unexpected News

'Lovely pair of shoes, lovely pair of shoes,' teased Leroy once they were out of the preacher's earshot.

'Shut up, Leroy!' Sandra aimed a kick at Leroy with her pointed toes. She missed but Leroy got the message.

'War declared!' commented her Uncle Bertie who had been standing behind them. He was their father's brother and, though younger by some ten years, reminded Sandra of him. He was a bachelor and lived in the nearby village but nearly every Sunday he rode over on his bicycle to have lunch with them. Sometimes he came in time for church, if only to please Granny.

A party, including old Miss Simpson, the postmistress, and friends and neighbours and their children, often came back to the house to have some light refreshments and exchange gossip before leaving to prepare their Sunday dinners.

This was one of the only times that Granny entertained friends and it was usually a happy occasion filled with chatter and laughter.

Granny would read out the letters from England with relish from behind her horn-rimmed spectacles which she put on for the occasion. She had elevated these letter-reading sessions into a fine art, pausing for dramatic effect or repeating a phrase at the right moment or stopping and adding comments of her own when occasion demanded.

'Any news from England?' probed Uncle Bertie.

'Everybody fine the last time I hear,' said Granny. They all assumed that Granny hadn't received a letter so there were sighs of disappointment all round. Again Sandra wondered about the letter she had seen Granny hide.

11

'Bertie, I have some nice ice-cream mixture.' It was Granny's way of asking him to go and buy some ice from the ice factory on the outskirts of the town.

It was the cue for Leroy to take out his bicycle and for Sandra to beg to be allowed to hitch a ride with him.

'Not in your Sunday clothes,' shouted Granny from the kitchen, but both Leroy and Sandra had anticipated her words, and had already changed into T-shirts and shorts and plimsolls.

'Mind how you go!' counselled Granny as they set off down the road with Uncle Bertie. Sandra sat on the crossbar of Leroy's bike with her hands planted firmly on the handlebars between his.

In about fifteen minutes they reached the ice factory. Inside was like a massive refrigerator with slabs of ice of varying sizes piled up one on top of the other. Uncle Bertie bought a small slab and rested it on one of the handlebars of his bicycle. He waited for a few moments for the ice to melt and form a groove around the handlebar to prevent it from slipping off. He mounted the bike and rode along precariously. One hand held the ice slab in place while he steered with the other. It was a miracle that neither he nor the ice fell off.

Granny was ready with the ice-cream bucket and the mixture as they had to work fast to make the ice cream before the ice melted. The creamy mixture, flavoured with fresh mango, was poured in the metal container at the centre of the bucket. Bertie closed the container and packed chipped ice round its sides. Coarse salt was sprinkled on top of the ice to lower the temperature.

Everybody, excepting the older men and women, took turns to spin the handle of the bucket, churning the mixture round and round, till magically it would thicken into delicious ice cream. It was always Granny's privilege to taste the mixture to decide if it was finished, and she never failed to delay the proceedings by announcing that it wasn't quite finished yet. This time was no different.

'Come, Granny, taste it and tell us if it ready,' called Leroy.

Granny came with her wooden spoon. She tasted the mixture and deliberated for a moment. 'It still have a far way to go.'

'Shucks, Granny, we going starve to death before this ice cream ready.'

'Lazy crab never get fat,' was Granny's reply.

So Leroy, then Sandra, then Uncle Bertie churned.

'It must ready now,' said Uncle Bertie, wiping beads of perspiration from his forehead.

'It need just a little more churning,' said Granny. 'Just a little more.'

'Lord have mercy,' said Uncle Bertie. 'I can see you don't like ice cream no more.'

'Chu,' said Granny, 'you love your belly too much!'

'But a empty sack can't stand up, you know, Ma'.'

'And you not letting us forget that a empty vessel mek the most noise!'

'Tell him, Ma James, tell him!' Everybody laughed heartily at Granny's triumph over her son. They all knew that Granny was being much too fussy, but didn't at all mind because the churning was as much fun as the eating.

After a further round of vigorous churning Uncle Bertie challenged her, 'Tell me it not ready now!'

Granny tasted, considered, tasted again and said with a flourish, 'Now it ready.'

There was loud applause. Sandra fetched the cones.

'Not so fast, young lady,' said Granny. 'You have to wait a few minutes for it to set.'

Sandra always forgot about the wretched setting time. These were always the longest minutes. At last however the delicious ice cream was being scooped up into cones and handed around. When the last of the ice cream was served, Sandra and Leroy always fought over the container, cleaning it out with their fingers then meticulously licking them clean.

It wasn't till after the guests had eaten their full and drained the last of the sorrel and cream soda and rum from their glasses, told Granny what a wonderful time they had had and had finally left (except Uncle Bertie who was staying for lunch), that the mystery of the letter was cleared up.

Leroy and Uncle Bertie were busy outside, clearing up and putting away the ice-cream bucket. Granny was seated on her easy chair on the front veranda.

'Sandra . . .'

'Yes, Granny?'

'I have some news for you.'

'News, Granny?'

'Yes,' she said, producing the letter and donning her spectacles. 'You going to England.'

The news came as a shock. It had always been the plan for Leroy to go first as he was older, though Sandra had been hoping that her parents would have been able to raise enough money for them to travel up at the same time. Better still she had hoped that by some miracle her mother and father would come back to Jamaica, for she wanted no more goodbyes, no more tearful farewells.

'Me, Granny?'

'Is how many Sandras live in this house?' teased Granny.

For a moment Sandra felt a flush of happiness. All she could think of was that she was going to see her mother and father again and meet the twins.

Then she thought of Leroy and felt ashamed of her own happiness. Poor Leroy. How must he be feeling?

'I thought they would send for Leroy first,' said Sandra.

'When a girl reach your age she need her mother. Me too old now to be responsible for a twelve-year-old girl.'

It was now Sandra's turn to taste the cup of rejection.

'So you sending me away, and keeping Leroy,' she accused half-jokingly.

' "Alligator lay egg, but him not fowl", so don't look at things from one side only.'

The discussion was cut short when Leroy came on to the veranda. He avoided Sandra's gaze. Sandra realised at once that Uncle Bertie must have told him.

At length Uncle Bertie joined the silent group. Even his usual

14

jovial presence didn't relieve the awkward silence that lay between them like a shattered drum.

Finally it was Granny who spoke with feeling: 'I don't know why your father ever pick himself up and go to England.'

3 The Passport Photo

'Now don't forget to smile when he take the picture,' advised Granny as the bus approached. 'For when they open your passport in England, I want them to see a nice smiling face. I want them to . . .'

Sandra was relieved that Granny's words were drowned by the approaching bus. It had a sign, IN GOD WE TRUST, emblazoned on its side and as usual was being driven by Catboy. How he came to be called Catboy was a mystery, but he had won favour as a driver of style, the length and breadth of the parish because of his skill in double-declutching as he changed gears and the exuberance of his horn-blowing. Amidst the hissing of air-brakes he gave the horn several sharp jabs in rapid succession like a roll of drums, followed by a long sustained note like the end of a Louis Armstrong number.

'Listen to that Catboy, eh,' one of the waiting women said in admiration. 'He think he playing in a band fer true!'

Granny tut-tutted under her teeth to signal that she did not approve of all that exhibitionism. She thought it a good idea if they 'killed two birds with one stone' and had Leroy's passport photo taken as well. At first she was mortified that Leroy didn't have a proper suit in which to be photographed, but in the end was reconciled to the idea of his wearing a shirt and tie.

Sandra and Leroy boarded the bus and Granny came round to the side and chatted with them through the open side window while the driver waited for the other passengers to settle down, mostly women on their way to market. A woman at the back of the bus struggled with two mesh-wire boxes full of clucking hens. Outside, the sideman loaded boxes of bananas and oranges and yams and sweet potatoes and every imaginable type of vegetable, on to the top of the bus.

'Make sure they get off at the right stop. I don't want them to end up in Runaway Bay,' shouted Granny to the conductress as Catboy revved up the engine and gave a few sharp blasts of the horn to warn stragglers that the journey was about to begin.

The face of the conductress creased with amusement. 'Is all right, lady, we not going further than Ochi,' she said.

'Granny knew that!' fumed Sandra under her breath, poking Leroy with her elbows. Leroy just chuckled and shook his head.

As they waved to Granny from the bus she shouted one parting piece of advice: 'The devil find work for idle hands so don't dilly-dally in town when you finish, come straight back home!'

'Yes, Granny!' they shouted and waved cheerfully to her as the bus pulled away.

They settled back in the seat. Sandra was overcome by a sense of freedom and happiness, as if they were setting off on a holiday excursion instead of travelling twenty miles to have their photographs taken.

She was decked out in her best dress with its sleeveless scoop neck and a full-length skirt with lace trim round the hem. Her hair was parted in the middle and drawn up into two tight plaits which were secured by cheerful yellow ribbons. The ribbons made her look much too girlish, she thought, but Granny had bought them specially, and she hadn't wished to offend her by not wearing them. Otherwise Sandra was quite happy with her appearance and was careful in her movements, anxious not to get her dress ruffled too much by the rough and tumble of the bus ride.

She even managed to smile for the photographer.

'Come back at two o'clock and your pictures will be ready,' he said.

They had four hours to kill and spent some time wandering around the town. More shops, restaurants and bars had sprung up since they were last there and they noticed more American tourists looking faintly ridiculous in their obligatory uniform of Bermuda shorts, colourful short-sleeved shirt, straw hat and

17

camera. There was even an art gallery. They enjoyed looking at the paintings of market women and fishermen and tropical landscapes. They wandered around the craft markets which were teeming with the hustle and bustle of vendors selling the same straw goods and wooden carvings and other hackneyed souvenirs.

Groups of men lounged idly outside rum shops or cafés while from inside the familiar sound of noisy domino games in progress – thump, thump, thump – pierced the air. In the main street a record shop played all the latest hits as loudly as it dared.

Sandra and Leroy were startled by a barefooted character walking along the road, who entertained onlookers by beating out rhythms on his face and body. With the bare palms of his hands he struck his cheeks and bare chest with such ferocity that the sound echoed like the taut skin of a drum and could be heard from some distance.

'Poor fellow,' said Sandra.

'He must be mad,' said Leroy.

'That must really hurt,' said Sandra shuddering.

'If teacher give him a beating at school, he wouldn't even feel it,' speculated Leroy chuckling.

Sandra thrust her hand in her purse and took out a shilling. 'Here, Leroy, give this to him.'

'Why you giving him money, Sandra?'

'He look so poor, Leroy. He must be hungry.'

'Don't be stupid, Sandra. Leave that to the tourists.'

But the man had seen Sandra take the money from her purse and came over and held out one hand while continuing the drumming with the other. Sandra put the shilling in his outstretched hand. He pocketed the money and resumed the two-hand drumming with hardly a glance at her.

'See, he didn't even say thanks,' said Leroy.

Sandra was a bit peeved by his ingratitude, but she wasn't about to admit that to Leroy. 'You can't do things just to get thanks.'

'Well, better your lunch money than mine.'

'Talking about lunch, Leroy, my belly hungry.'

18

They had a light lunch of bottled soft drinks and peppery patties while sitting on a wall facing the tranquil bay. By now the sun was at its fiercest. It cast deep shadows under the eyes of those whose business brought them out into the streets away from the protection of louvre-windowed houses or offices cooled by large overhead fans. Leroy and Sandra were grateful for the pool of shade cast by the broad leaves of an almond tree whose branches spread like an umbrella above them.

Because Sandra had given away a shilling, she had one patty less than Leroy, and had finished eating before him. He was just about to bite into his extra patty when his eyes met hers.

'Serve you right for throwing away your good money.'

Sandra sucked her teeth.

'Anyway, I take pity on you.' He smiled as he broke the patty in two and gave her a piece.

They went to collect the photos on the dot of two o'clock. The photographer handed them a sealed envelope. They paid him and hurried outside to scrutinise the photos but they heard the horn announcing Catboy's imminent departure. They ran as fast as they could to catch the bus.

As the bus belched and stuttered down the road, Leroy opened the window to let in some fresh air, but the incoming air was like a blast from a furnace. He slumped back in his seat.

'You not going look at the pictures?' he queried.

'Oh yes,' said Sandra, suddenly realising that she had been absent-mindedly using the envelope as a fan.

'You didn't bust the camera after all,' said Leroy looking at the photos over her shoulders.

'Go away, Leroy,' said Sandra smiling. She was pleased with her photos – the first of her on her own. Granny would be pleased about the smile, she thought.

'Let me see,' said Leroy.

Leroy's mood in his photograph was restrained, but he had a faint smile. Sandra thought that the photographs might be a mirror of their current states of mind: she, on the brink of major changes in her life, seemed full of confidence and optimism, while

Leroy's expression seemed passive, even forlorn. She felt the same pangs of guilt she had first felt when she knew that she and not Leroy was going to England.

'I wish you was coming with me.' She had not yet spoken to him about her going.

Leroy smiled and gazed out of the window.

'It would be nice, wouldn't it, eh, Leroy?' she asked, trying again.

'Maybe . . .'

'An' we could be all together again.'

'I suppose so,' said Leroy.

'What you mean, you suppose so?'

'Everybody want to look life in England, but Jamaica have life too.'

'Lots of things you can do in England that you can't do here,' said Sandra with conviction, though she wasn't at all sure what those things were.

'And lots of things you can do in Jamaica that you can't do in England,' countered Leroy.

Sandra had never looked at it that way. So many people were jostling to join the queue to get into England that it tended to obscure the good things about Jamaica. Still, she couldn't quite believe that Leroy wouldn't prefer to be reunited with his family. Maybe he was just trying to make her feel less guilty.

'I bet it's Angela,' she teased, deliberately lightening the mood.

'Who . . .?'

'You heard me. Angela Douglas.'

'What you mean?'

'You can't say you don't like her . . .'

'She's all right.'

'An' you don't want to leave her behind . . .'

'I didn't say so.'

'I'm saying so.'

'You just chatting foolishness.'

'I see you with her every day after school . . .'

'She's a nice girl but there are lots of other fish in the sea.'

20

'I didn't know you so interested in fishing,' Sandra said with as much sarcasm as she could muster.

'I just don't have time for any girlfriend yet,' said Leroy defensively.

Granny was always warning him about taking up with girls before he finished his exams. Perhaps he was heeding her words, Sandra thought.

Granny was waiting for them at the bus stop when they got to the village. She was pleased with the photos.

'You look good even though you don't have on a jacket,' she said to Leroy. 'But why you couldn't put on a bigger smile, eh?'

She looked at Sandra's photos. 'What a way you look nice,' she exclaimed. 'And such a lovely smile.'

Granny smiled as if competing with the photographs.

4 'My granddaughter going to England'

Sandra now had only one month to prepare for her departure. One month to get used to the idea of living in a strange land.

Somehow the photographs her mother and father sent back didn't match the image of England in school books: quaint thatched cottages and pretty rose gardens and picturesque villages and old castles and palaces and pomp and ceremony. In the photographs their winter clothes seemed strange and oppressive and the surroundings grey and unfriendly.

All Sandra knew was the warmth of the Jamaican climate and she found it difficult to imagine why anyone should ever need to wear a thick overcoat over layers and layers of clothes.

The following Sunday when they were making ice cream again, she placed the palm of her hand on the block of ice and held it there for as long as she dared, trying to feel what it would be like to live in a cold country. Her hand went quite numb and pained a little, but it was quite bearable. She couldn't understand what all the fuss was about and she was sure she would never need to wear gloves when she went to live in England. But when the parcel arrived containing two thick jumpers, a heavy black overcoat and a pair of woollen gloves, she changed her mind.

Under the watchful eyes of Granny and Leroy, she tried on one of the jumpers.

'Turn round, let me see,' said Granny who would pronounce final judgement on the fit. 'Just right,' she said.

'The sleeves too long, Granny,' moaned Sandra.

'It's just right,' countermanded Granny, 'for you don't want a "just fit". You want clothes that have room for you to grow into.

These clothes cost too much for you to wear for one winter and then they can't fit you after that.'

Granny went up to Sandra and folded the sleeve of the jumper so that it was just the right length.

'See, I tell you is the right fit.'

Sandra then fitted the overcoat. It wasn't just the sleeves that were too big. It was too big all over. She was miserable.

'What you screwing up your face for, child?'

Sandra didn't want to appear ungrateful.

'By the time you put on all your winter clothes and your jumper under it, it will be a perfect fit.'

The thought of having to wear so many layers of clothes filled Sandra with dismay.

The best part of going away was the shopping. Her parents had sent money for those clothes she would need on the trip, like shoes which needed to be fitted properly and summer clothes.

So one bright Saturday morning at the crack of dawn, Granny and Sandra set off by bus to Kingston, leaving Leroy behind. Granny maintained that only the capital would do for such an important shopping expedition, though it was a long and tortuous trip by bus. Sandra didn't mind for she had rarely visited Kingston.

Their first port of call was the Bata shoe shop. The manager served them personally. He was a dapper little man dressed in a neat suit and tie with a red carnation on his jacket lapel.

'My granddaughter going to England and need a nice pair of shoes.'

'Would mademoiselle care to try these?' he asked, selecting the best shoes on display.

Granny had a quick look at the price. 'Those are a bit fancy.'

'These would show off the elegance of mademoiselle's slender feet,' he said, selecting another pair, equally expensive.

It amused and flattered Sandra to be called 'mademoiselle', but Granny was determined not to be overwhelmed by the sweet talk of slick city folk.

'She need a good strong pair of shoes that can withstand

snow and rain. These wouldn't last a day in England,' she said, inspecting the shoes.

The manager raised his eyebrows.

'England not like Jamaica, you know,' Granny added, with the triumphant air of someone administering the final *coup de grâce*. Granny was rapidly becoming an expert on England and all things English. 'My son in England six years now,' she added with pride, for it added weight to her pronouncements on that country.

'I have just the pair in mind, madame!' intoned the manager with professional coolness under fire and before long Sandra was trying on the first of what turned out to be a succession of shoes. Although the manager had carefully measured Sandra's feet and supervised the fittings, Granny always pinched the tip of the shoes to ensure that there was enough space for her growing feet.

'I don't want my granddaughter to get no corn or bunion on her feet,' she explained to the manager.

Had it not been for the diplomatic skills and salesmanship of the manager, Sandra would have left with a pair of shoes that were more to Granny's taste than her own and two sizes too big at that.

'Would to God every customer were like you, madame,' pronounced the manager, bowing politely to Granny as they left the shop.

'That man talk like him have hot potato in him mouth with him madame this and mademoiselle that!' chuckled Granny when they were out of earshot.

Then it was off to the clothes shop.

'My granddaughter is going to England and we come to buy some nice dress for her to wear. You have any nice dress?'

That put the assistant on the defensive and put Granny firmly in the driving seat. Before the assistant could respond Granny added: 'She is my big son daughter, you know. He and his wife in England and they send for her.' Granny was unashamedly basking in the shade of Sandra's reflected glory.

'What size is your granddaughter?'

'She is a size ten now but she growing fast.' Sandra knew

exactly what that meant. Granny, of course, played an active role in the selection and fitting of the clothes, standing back to appraise the effect.

'Ah want her to arrive in England looking her best. You mus' always mek a good impression wherever you go,' counselled Granny to no one in particular.

After Granny had fussed over the quality of material, appraised their style and fittings and haggled over prices, they left with Sandra clutching a bag with three dresses, a set of underclothes, pyjamas and socks.

'Now we have to get you a hat,' said Granny.

'A hat?' protested Sandra.

'You turning into a young lady now and you should wear a hat when you go to church.'

So it was off to the hat shop. After trying on a series of hats, Sandra settled for a narrow-rimmed grey hat, which, in Granny's opinion, would create the right impression in England.

Sandra was exhausted by the day's outing and fell asleep in the bus going home, resting her head on Granny's shoulder. It was pitch dark by the time they arrived home.

5 Farewells

The worst part about leaving was saying goodbye to her school friends. Lorna was her best friend. They were in the same class and spent most of their free time at school together. Sometimes they joined in playground games with other children, but as the time for her departure neared Sandra spent more and more time with her.

The school was on a hill overlooking the sea. During breaks Sandra and Lorna would find the shade of the poinciana tree dominated the playground. They would sit and gaze in silence at the far-off horizon.

One day they spotted the faint outline of an ocean liner silently gliding across the sea to some far-off destination, and their thoughts sailed to England.

'When you coming back?' asked Lorna.

'I don't know.'

'Will you be away a long time?'

'I don't know.'

'How you mean, you don't know?'

It was a question that Sandra found difficult to answer. She had not really thought about it. It was difficult, too, because she no longer knew how long 'long' was.

'Perhaps I won't come back at all,' said Sandra with sudden dismay, as the possibility suddenly occurred to her.

'Never come back!'

'Not for a long time anyway. Just think how much money it would cost . . .'

Lorna said nothing. They listened in silence to the distant roar of the sea as the waves crashed against the shore. A gentle breeze rustled the leaves of the poinciana tree.

'Maybe I could go to England too,' said Lorna.

'Maybe,' said Sandra without encouraging the thought, for she knew that Lorna was living happily at home with her family. How could she begin to tell her that, amidst all the excitement of leaving, there was also pain and heartbreak.

'Yes, you could come and live near to me,' continued Sandra with more hope.

'And we could go to the same school and be in the same class,' added Lorna enthusiastically.

They watched as the faint outline of the ship disappeared over the horizon. Then Sandra spotted one of the black sword-shaped pods that had fallen from the poinciana tree. She reached and picked it up. When she shook it, it made a rattling noise like the shakers used by calypso bands. She sang to the accompaniment of the pod:

Mamma, lend me your pigeon to keep company with mine,
Mamma, lend me your pigeon to keep company with mine.
Me pigeon gone wild in the bush, me pigeon gone wild,
Me pigeon gone wild in the bush, me pigeon gone wild.

Lorna joined in and they sang it again, over and over.

'Last one to the sea is a dog!' said Sandra, suddenly getting up, running as fast as she could. Lorna chased her as they raced down to the edge of the playing fields, skipped over tufts of tall grass that skirted the beach and finally on to the beach itself, although it was strictly out of bounds during school hours.

They threw off their shoes and gathered up their skirts between their legs as they played barefooted hide-and-seek with the waves which crashed on the shore and chased their feet with foaming, hissing playfulness. They shrieked with delight when the waves tricked them with a sudden swelling and breaking that caught them unawares and soaked the hems of their uniforms.

Finally exhausted, they fell to the beach a safe distance from the frothy tentacles of the seas. They watched as the waves washed up and spitefully flooded their footprints. When the waves subsided the sand was left flat and clear, and their footprints had disappeared – like the blackboard after the teacher had wiped it clean.

'Chu, the sea always wins in the end,' said Sandra ruefully as they heard the school bell summoning them back to the classroom.

At long last the eve of Sandra's departure arrived. More and more friends and relatives dropped by to bid her farewell, bringing gifts. Granny busied herself making light refreshments for the visitors in between packing for Sandra and fussing over her.

Many of her school friends called.

'You are lucky to be going to England,' said one.

'I wish I was going,' said another.

'I hear the streets of England paved with gold.'

'You must send some gold for us,' teased another.

The most unexpected visitor was Mrs Beckford, their neighbour, whose husband had died and left her a widow long ago. She had not spoken to Granny for years because there was bad blood between them. She turned up bearing gifts. Granny was as shocked to see her as was Sandra.

'I come to say goodbye to Sandra and give her a little something.'

Granny stood speechless for a moment before recovering her composure.

'You come just in time, Ma Becky,' said Granny, 'for she leaving tomorrow.'

Granny was just making polite conversation because she knew well that Ma Becky would have known all the details, even down to the hour of Sandra's departure. News and gossip had a way of beating a path to Ma Becky's ears.

'I bring her a few mangoes for her trip on the ship.'

Granny couldn't help but laugh. It was a laugh which was aimed at burying the hatchet. Ma Becky joined in the laughter as well and so did Sandra and Leroy.

'Come in and sit down,' said Granny.

Two years ago, Sandra and Leroy had raided Ma Becky's

mango tree. For weeks they watched the mangoes on the tree near the fence which divided the two yards ripen and swell. One big juicy mango in particular attracted their attention. Every day they looked to see if Ma Becky would pick it. But she didn't. She hardly showed any interest in it, and finally the mango, laden with sweetness, dropped to the ground. And there it lay for two days, till others joined it. It was more than Sandra and Leroy could bear. One afternoon, when they thought Ma Becky was resting, they scaled the fence and crept up on the mangoes.

Leroy stuffed his pockets with two of the biggest ones and Sandra collected four in the folds of her skirt. They were just about to return to safety when they heard Ma Becky's voice: 'Is who tell oonoo to tek me mangoes dem?'

They froze. Sandra let her hands go and the mangoes tumbled to the ground. Leroy dropped his load too.

'Answer me!' insisted Ma Becky. 'Is who tell oonoo to come eena me yard in broad daylight and thief me mangoes, eh?'

'We never think you want them, Ma Becky,' answered Leroy.

'So fe you granny don't have money to buy you mangoes at the market, eh? Don't she get money from her rich son in England?'

She knew Granny would hear and she was going for the jugular.

Granny flew into a rage and came out blazing. But tactically she had first to distance herself from the misdemeanours of Leroy and Sandra and so she rounded on them. 'Put every one of those mangoes back! Is not any and everybody yard you can waltz into and pick up their mango, you know! Some people more mean and stingy than others and rather see their mangoes drop to the ground and rotten than see anybody eat it.'

'Your granpickney dem don't have no brought-upsy!' chided Ma Becky.

'Just watch that mouth of yours, Ma Becky,' warned Granny, pitching herself into the fray. 'I ain't 'fraid of you, you know.'

'Is not me, is prison you should be 'fraid of,' rejoined Ma Becky, 'because that's where them granpickney of yours going end up!'

'Some people shouldn't talk, because they turn their own house and yard into a prison.'

That started Ma Becky off. 'What I have in this house, you would never dream of having, no matter how long you live.' Ma Becky then disappeared inside her house and returned with a crystal decanter. 'You have crystal decanter, eh?'

She paused, waiting for an answer which she knew wouldn't come because she knew Granny could hardly afford to buy wine, let alone a crystal decanter in which to store it.

Emboldened by her first taste of victory, Ma Becky brought out a small kitchen table. 'You have Formica kitchen table?'

Granny was sullen.

Once again Ma Becky returned inside and this time she lugged her sewing machine on to the veranda. 'You have Singer electric sewing-machine?'

By now Ma Becky knew that Granny was defeated. So, assured of final victory, Ma Becky went to and fro from house to veranda, fetching and carrying every little artefact that could possibly inspire jealousy. Each item she put down was like a dagger in Granny's heart.

At length Ma Becky stood triumphant, hands akimbo, in front of her possessions, which now lined the entire steps and veranda. It looked like the display window of a shop that was holding a clearing sale.

'Answer me, Ma James, you have any of these things?' And satisfied that no answer was forthcoming, she started to list the things, one by one again. It had now become a twisted, compulsive game, replayed for the benefit of the audience that had gathered to witness such a compelling piece of theatre.

'Ma Becky mad for true!' said an onlooker.

'Fancy shaming Ma James so!' said another.

'An' in front of her grandchildren! Ma Becky too out of order, yu' hear!'

Granny, who had watched in silence throughout, took some comfort from the sympathy of the crowd and broke the spell at last.

'Possession is not everything,' she said. And raising her voice, not so much for Ma Becky but for the audience, she added: 'For it is easier for a camel to pass through the eye of a needle than for a rich man to enter the kingdom of heaven!'

The Bible had come to Granny's rescue. With a defiant little toss of her head, she turned her back on Ma Becky and headed back inside with Sandra and Leroy in tow.

'And some people going to rot in hell because of too much possession!' she shouted as a parting shot.

The crowd roared their approval and loudly applauded Granny.

Ma Becky shamefacedly began the laborious task of returning the possessions inside the house.

Sandra was overcome by a mixture of pride and shame. She felt pride in Granny's stout defence of herself and Leroy, but shame in the poverty that so nearly bowed Granny's head. She swore that she would never be poor when she grew up. That one day she would have enough money to buy Granny a big house and a Singer sewing-machine and a Formica table and all the things that she could ever want.

And now, after two years of silence and bad blood between the two women, Ma Becky had taken the first step to bury the hatchet. Sandra was glad that Granny had accepted Ma Becky's gesture. She knew that both Granny and Ma Becky would benefit from being friends again.

'Thank you for the mangoes, Ma Becky,' said Sandra, accepting the gift with her best smile. She placed them in a box which Granny had put aside for food for the voyage.

She continued with last-minute packing while Granny and Ma Becky sat down and sipped cool drinks as they tried to pick up the pieces of their broken friendship. After a while Ma Becky returned home but not before cuddling Sandra and kissing both her cheeks as if nothing had ever happened to sour the relations between them.

The last person to say goodbye was Lorna. She had come in the morning and spent all day with Sandra, helping her with her packing. At twilight she prepared to go home.

'I have a present for you,' she said, holding out a necklace. It was a string of beads she had made from the poinciana pods from the school tree.

'That's the best present I ever had,' said Sandra with feeling. 'I will keep it to remember you by.'

Then Lorna had disappeared into the growing darkness of the night, leaving Sandra with a heavy heart.

She had an overwhelming feeling of excitement but an undercurrent of melancholy kept her excitement in check. She had had the same mix of feeling before, when they had left the family house to come to live with Granny. It was worse then because the house had been emptied of every familiar thing and had lost its spirit. But now she had to say goodbye to prized possessions like her dresses and school books. She felt unexpected affection, too, for Granny's hens and ducks and goats and even the shaggy stray cat that she occasionally fed scraps of food.

'Can I take Lizzie with me, Granny?' she asked when her eyes fell on the oversize doll that had been her companion for the last six years.

'You too old for dolls now,' replied Granny, 'and in any case you don't have no space in your suitcase.'

'I could take her in a plastic bag, Granny?'

'There are many rivers to cross in this life,' said Granny, 'and sometimes you have to lighten your load to get across.'

Sandra was silent for a while. She thought about all the friends that she had said goodbye to, and she thought about Leroy and Granny too. She consoled herself with the thought that people are more important than dolls. But it didn't take away the pain and for a while she sulked.

'Is time to wash you hair,' pronounced Granny.

They went to the cistern in the outhouse, leaving Leroy to finish packing the food Sandra was taking aboard the ship and to write a letter to their parents for Sandra to deliver. Granny turned on the tap and thoroughly wetted her hair before applying the gel from the fleshy stem of a recently cut aloe vera plant. Granny swore by this home-grown shampoo. She rubbed the slimy gel into Sandra's hair till it lathered to a soapy consistency.

Back in the front room, Granny sat on the stool and Sandra,

accustomed to the ritual, sat on the floor at her feet while Granny dried her hair. Resting her back against Granny's parted knees, Sandra leant her head back and submitted to the vigorous movements of the towel. Granny's coarse working hands were transformed into tender caring ones as she massaged coconut oil into the roots of Sandra's hair with the tips of her fingers before spreading the oil to the rest of her hair with the palms of her hands.

With a wide-toothed comb, Granny parted her hair into tufts then expertly wove them into myriad plaits. To avoid pulling and hurting, each tuft had to be free from any knots, particularly at the tips. But she never succeeded in avoiding pain, and the pain in turn acted as a kind of bond between them. There was a time when Sandra would have screamed but she was too old for that now. Granny plaited her hair into tight plaits, so tight that she felt her scalp tingle, but she knew that by the morning it would be perfect.

'Sometimes I think we women take all the pain in the world on to weself,' she said to Sandra.

The washing and drying and plaiting of Sandra's hair always served as a mask for Granny's love. Whatever feeling of affection Granny felt for Leroy and Sandra had never found expression in hugs or kisses. Instead Granny would show her love by buying little gifts or cooking special meals for them or nursing them when they were sick or even in administering the dreaded doses of castor oil.

They put Sandra's luggage neatly by the front door to await Mr Mullings, who would take her and her luggage in his old black Dodge to Kingston as he had done for her mother and father.

'Goodnight, Granny,' she said at length.

Granny stood facing her. She seemed uncertain as to what to say, as if it had just occurred to her that it was Sandra's last night in Jamaica.

'Goodnight, darling,' she said before abruptly turning and retiring to bed. Sandra couldn't ever recall Granny calling her 'darling'.

6 Moonlight

Try as she might Sandra couldn't sleep.

She covered her ears with her pillow to block out the music that drifted up from the nearby club. Yet the deep muffled throb of the bass guitar, steady and rhythmic like her own heartbeat, penetrated the tropical night, seeped through the wooden structure of the house, through the feathery defences of her pillow and invaded her consciousness.

The music was as much a part of the night as the whistling toads, chirping crickets and barking dogs that filled the air, too much a part of the fabric of her life to disturb her. Of course, it must have been the thought that this was her last night in Jamaica that kept her awake.

Sandra opened her eyes. The moonlight filtered through the cracks in the louvre window and came to rest on the flaxen hair of Lizzie as she cuddled her. She agreed that at twelve she was too old for dolls, but Lizzie reminded her of England and her father. She remembered the excitement when the postman brought the big parcel with the postmark London, England, stamped on it. She couldn't wait to tear off the brown paper and see what was inside. It was the biggest doll she had ever seen. It stood in a box covered with a film of cellophane, staring at her through wide round blue eyes: blue eyes warmed by the smile that creased its cherub-like cheeks.

Sandra remembered how she had hugged the doll and kissed her and saw, not a golden fairy princess, but the smiling black face of her father. And she loved him all the more.

Sandra was lurched back to the present by the sound of Granny in the adjoining bedroom. She heard the shuffle of slippered feet as she made her way to the door, the floorboards creaking beneath her weight.

She heard the door of her bedroom open and she turned quickly on her side and closed her eyes. She pretended to be asleep, allowing her breath to deepen, releasing it with a forced rasping sigh. She sensed the hovering figure of Granny appraising the situation. Sandra furtively opened an eye and peeped out at Granny. The moonlight illuminated her face and exaggerated the whiteness of her hair. She looked ghostly and for a moment Sandra felt afraid.

But it was no ghost. It was Granny all right. She stood in the doorway, her hand resting lightly on the door frame, more in a gesture of contemplation than for support. She stood there for what seemed an eternity. Sandra continued to watch as Granny tilted her head and gazed at her with a mixture of affection, pride and sadness.

Then Granny made her way to the louvre window and closed the shutters. Granny had warned her time and again: 'You will get a crick neck if you sleep with the moonlight on your face.' Some folk believed though that it was because the moonlight could bewitch you, and Sandra was never sure which one Granny really believed. The room darkened and Sandra heard her shuffle back to her bedroom, moving even more slowly in the darkness. Sandra felt a stab of guilt for her little deception, but she knew that Granny would only fuss if she discovered that she was awake. She pulled Lizzie close to her and her thoughts floated across the ocean to England. She was so lost in her thoughts that she was startled to discover that the music had stopped. The night now fully belonged to the whistling toads and the chirping crickets and the dogs that barked from time to time.

Sandra reminded herself that she had to be up bright and early in the morning. Her thoughts settled on the frilly white dress Granny had laid out on the chair at the foot of the bed, and the new pair of shoes that she would wear for the first time.

And so, distracted by thoughts of what she was going to wear, she drifted into a deep sleep.

7 Granny's Grace

Sandra woke at the crack of dawn. But Granny and Leroy were already up and about. The breakfast table was set and laden with an enormous feast, as if Granny was convinced that Sandra might starve on board the ship so was taking the precaution of fattening her up.

There was cornmeal porridge, a mountain of scrambled eggs and fried plantains and generous slices of buttered bread as well as toasted cassava wafers. As always there was a jar of Granny's home-made guava jelly.

'You better eat it all up,' advised Granny from the kitchen, 'because it hard to find this kind of food in England, you know.'

'Don't worry, Granny, I won't need to eat for a month after this,' said Sandra, rubbing her tummy in anticipation.

Granny removed her apron and joined them at the table.

'Now let us grace the table,' she said getting suddenly serious.

Leroy and Sandra braced themselves. On important family occasions, Granny's grace could easily stretch into a sermon.

'Almighty God, our Heavenly Father, we thank you for the gift of this food you spread before us, and for making us hale and hearty enough to enjoy it. We also remember in our prayers those who are too poor to have enough food to eat. We pray for your blessings on Sandra's endeavour as she cross the sea to be with her parents who she don't set eyes on for a good while now. We pray that she will have a safe trip and not get into any mischief on board ship and bring shame on the James name.'

'Amen,' said Leroy.

'I'm not finished yet, Leroy,' said Granny, opening her eyes

36

and peering at him over the rim of her glasses. Granny took a deep breath and continued.

'We offer up special prayers for her mother and father and the twins in England, and pray that Sandra will arrive in England safe and that she will find them in good health. We pray that Sandra will trust and lean on Your everlasting arm, for Your mercy endureth ever faithful, ever sure. We pray that in the fullness of time Leroy will be united with his family in England, even if I going to miss him as much as I going to miss Sandra. We pray this in Jesus name. Amen.'

'Amen,' said Leroy and Sandra in unison, after a moment's pause to satisfy themselves that Granny had well and truly finished, then immediately tucked into the food. For a while there was only the sound of knives and forks against plates.

'Have some more, Sandra,' urged Granny, spooning a second helping of ackees and saltfish on to her plate. Leroy didn't stand on ceremony and extended his plate for seconds too.

'You had a nice sleep?' queried Granny.

'Yes, Granny.'

Granny fussed over Sandra for the rest of the meal, right up to the time they raised their glasses and drank their milky soursop punch.

'Delicious,' said Sandra.

Mr Mullings drew up in the old Dodge at the front gate promptly at seven a.m. He was a short dark stocky man dressed in a black suit and tie and holding a felt hat in his hand.

'Your timing is as good as ever, Mr Mullings,' complimented Granny.

'Well, I can't afford for the little English lady to miss her boat,' joked Mr Mullings.

Soon the luggage was packed into the back of the Dodge and they took their seats in the car with Granny up front with Mr Mullings and Leroy and Sandra at the back.

As they sped down the road, Sandra cast one last backward glance at the house, as if trying to fix it in her mind for future reference.

They drove along the coast before turning inland. The road

rose steeply to cross the mountains. Mr Mullings blew his horn on the approach to every corner to warn any oncoming vehicles.

'Is because the government pay road contractors by the mile that these roads have so much twist and turn,' he joked. 'The thiefing contractors mek sure dat the work last long long,' he added just to make sure Leroy and Sandra got the joke.

Their progress was slowed from time to time by a bus or an overloaded lorry struggling up the hill and Mr Mullings had to wait for the right moment to overtake.

Just as they neared the brow of the mountain they ran into a sudden torrential downpour which forced Mr Mullings to reduce his speed to little more than a crawl. The windscreen wipers of the old Dodge whipped backwards and forwards ferociously, fending off the salvoes of rainwater. Sandra wiped the rear door window with the inside of her hand, and through cupped hands she peered outside, but only saw a blur of blue-green vegetation. Then just as suddenly as it had started, the rain stopped and there were blue skies and bright sunshine again.

They rounded a final bend and got a panoramic view of the distant plains of Kingston below. The old Dodge cruised leisurely down to the road leading into Kingston. This road was level and bordered by fields of cane whose stalks rose up two metres on both sides of the road, and stretched as far as the eye could see. On a hilltop a little away from the road, and barely visible above the overgrowth of weed and thistles, stood the ruined foundations of a Great House that during slavery days had dominated the landscape. A light breeze blew and the green forest of cane stalks rustled ghostly in the morning breeze.

They passed through Kingston with its massed houses. They went round a corner and saw Kingston Harbour spread out before them, placid and flat as a pane of glass. Sandra reached over and took Leroy by the hand and clutched it as if she never wanted to let go. Sandra had surprised herself, for she was more likely to punch Leroy than to cuddle him. Yet she wasn't surprised that he held hers just as firmly as she held his.

'Thank God we reach safe,' said Granny.

Scores of stevedores in a frenzy of activity carted boxes and crates of all shapes and sizes in every direction. Towering winches lifted giant rope nets containing crates and other cargo, and swung them upwards and outwards, before setting them down again in the bellies of the ships that lined the wharf.

They were met by a representative of the *Santa Maria*, the Spanish liner Sandra was to sail in. He pointed her out, lying at anchor at the end of the dock. Sandra's luggage was collected and wheeled out of sight on a large trolley.

They were then ushered into a room with a fan revolving overhead. Sandra's passport and travel documents were inspected, then it was time to board the ship. She was given the number of her cabin and Sandra was pleased that Granny and Leroy were allowed to come with her.

They made their way up the ladder, a wobbly flight of steps, temporarily secured to the side of the ship. The ship seemed large and forbidding as they climbed up, clinging nervously to the rope railings. As she stepped on deck Sandra's stomach reached up to her mouth. She had now entered the kingdom of the sea where the heave and swell of the waves ruled supreme.

They cautiously made their way across the upper deck and down a series of narrow stairs to the cabin which Sandra was to share with another girl. She was surprised at how narrow and cramped it was. There was a bunk bed against the partition wall and opposite was a porthole through which the wharf below could be seen.

She wanted the top bunk but was disappointed that it already had a pile of books and some loose clothes on it. She glanced at the label on a suitcase in a corner of the cabin. 'Look, Granny, her name is Annette Lawson and she is from Trinidad. I never meet anybody from Trinidad before.'

'Is not you alone,' said Granny.

'That makes three of us,' added Leroy.

Granny surveyed the cabin. 'It small but it clean, and you have a travelling companion so everything should be all right,' she said with authority.

Sandra sat with Granny and Leroy on the edge of the bottom bunk, trying to postpone the moment when they would part.

'Sandra, you must promise to be a good girl on the trip. I don't want you mother and father to think I don't raise you right.'

'Yes, Granny.'

'And don't forget to write your granny when you get to England now.'

'No, Granny.'

'And remember to wrap up yourself nice and warm on the trip, for I don't want you to have to write and tell me you arrive in England with a cold, you hear.'

'Yes, Granny.'

'An' mek sure you keep this handy,' she said, handing Sandra a folded square of brown paper.

'What's this?' enquired Sandra, somewhat puzzled by the strange gift.

'Is just a piece of brown paper.'

'Brown paper, Granny? What for?'

'Seasickness.'

'Seasickness?' repeated Sandra, now thoroughly mystified.

'Yes, chile. If the sea get rough an' you feeling sick, all you have to do is put this under your blouse against your chest.'

'And that will stop seasickness?'

'Why you think I bring the brown paper all this way if it not going to stop seasickness?'

'Where you get that from, Granny?' chuckled Leroy.

'You don't worry your little head where I get that from.'

'That sound like some old wives' tale to me,' said Leroy, unable to stifle his laughter.

'You can laugh all you want, young man, but is not your belly going to knot up on the high seas!'

'But how you so sure it really work, Granny?' intervened Sandra.

'I wearing a piece right now,' announced Granny, patting her chest and rustling the hidden brown paper. 'Every time I have to go 'pon the high seas, I mek sure I have me piece of brown paper rest 'gainst me chest, and I never get seasick yet!'

Leroy smiled and winked at Sandra. The only time Granny

ever set foot on a ship was to say goodbye to her relatives leaving for England.

'So when turtle come out of the pond and say alligator blind, you better believe him!' continued Granny undaunted.

'All right, Granny, I'll keep it in a safe place,' said Sandra, trying her best to keep a straight face. She succeeded in doing so till her eye met Leroy's and they both burst out laughing.

'Oonoo can laugh all oonoo want now,' scolded Granny, 'but mek sure you don't lose it, for when rough sea tek' you, you will be well an' glad for it!'

There was a second call for all visitors to disembark. Sandra followed Granny and Leroy as they made their way to the ladder. Granny faced her to say goodbye.

'I don't know when these old eyes goin' see you again, chile.'

Sandra felt her throat tighten. She bit her lips.

Granny seemed uncertain as to what to do next. Sandra took the initiative and hugged Granny. This time Granny hugged her in return. 'Now you be a good girl. I don't want to hear anything bad about you in England.'

'Goodbye, Granny,' said Sandra. She was clinging to Granny as if she had only now realised that she was on a ship bound for England. She didn't want to leave after all.

'Hush, chile,' said Granny. 'And give Wayne and Jean a kiss for me and tell Mamma and Dadda that you have been a very good girl.'

Sandra hugged and kissed Leroy.

'Take it easy,' said Leroy.

She watched through glazed eyes as Granny and Leroy made their way down the ladder. It struck Sandra for the first time how frail Granny looked as she inched her way down the steps, clinging to the rope with one hand and to Leroy with the other.

At the dockside they were joined by Mr Mullings and together they stood and waved their farewells. Sandra waved as cheerily as she could. She was trying to raise her own spirits and to recapture the feeling of festivity of her father's leaving when she had stood where Granny stood, waving goodbye to him.

The ship's anchor was drawn up as the engine bellowed into

action and the entire ship shuddered. The ship's officer on the bridge shouted a series of orders to officers at the bow and the stern of the ship.

'All clear aft.' Sandra heard the reply.

'All clear aft, Skipper,' the officer relayed to the captain who stood in the wheelhouse.

'Full astern, two port.' The skipper gave the order and the voyage was officially under way. A tug boat secured to the bow of the ship started to lead the ship out of the harbour and into the wide lanes of the high seas.

Slowly, the waving figures of Granny, Leroy and Mr Mullings grew smaller and smaller. The ship now swayed lightly to the motion of the ocean, as it inched away from the dockside. Its massive engines spat and bellowed and filled the air with the smell of petrol and smoke fumes.

Sandra remembered the boats that she and Leroy used to make out of coconut husks, using the broad leaf of the sea almond for a sail. And how, once launched at the river's mouth, they would bob up and down on the short distance to the sea at the mercy of even the smallest ripple that could scuttle them and leave them rudderless in the face of the ocean.

She felt a sense of peril as she strained to get a last glimpse of Granny and Leroy. For the first time in her life she felt entirely alone.

She ran on shaky legs across the deck of the ship and down the winding series of steps that led to her cabin. Once inside, she threw herself on to her bunk and buried her head in the pillow. And then all the watery saltiness of the ocean flooded through her eyes.

PART TWO – CROSSING OVER

8 Annette

'How long you planning to lie on that bed moping?' enquired Annette in the friendliest of Trinidadian accents.

Sandra didn't answer but the faint smile that crossed her face was all the encouragement Annette needed. 'My name is Annette and I come from Trinidad.'

'I know,' said Sandra. 'I saw you name on your luggage.'

'And your name is Sandra. I knew from the time I boarded the ship at Port au Spain because your name was down on the cabin list.'

They were interrupted by loudspeakers which called all new passengers to come on deck with their life-jackets. Sandra was alarmed.

'It's just a drill they put you through in case of an emergency,' said Annette, managing to sound like an old hand at sea travel.

On the main deck, the ship's flags fluttered noisily. Before the drill, Sandra met the stewardess who was in charge of them.

'I'll be keep an eye on you two during the voyage, so don't get up to any mischief now,' she said in friendly voice. 'And if you need any help I'm the person to ask.'

After the life-saving drill, Annette took Sandra on a grand tour of the boat. She showed her the dining room and the table where they were going to sit. She took her through several small lounges and past a long saloon bar where groups of West Indian men sat drinking and chatting and playing cards and noisy games of dominoes.

'Let me show you the stern,' said Annette. 'That's the back of the ship or the aft,' she explained.

They made their way to the stern. The ship left behind a long frothy wake like an ever-widening highway. A chorus of seabirds hovered over the ship like scavengers waiting for some titbits to be thrown overboard.

'Birds followed us all the way from Trinidad to Jamaica,' said Annette. 'I ain't know how they does fly for so far.'

Next Annette took Sandra to the bow of the ship which was rising and falling with each swell of the ocean. Sandra grabbed the rail to steady herself.

'You'll soon get your sea legs,' said Annette, walking about unaided.

Sandra wasn't convinced. She felt the contents of her stomach lurch upwards towards her mouth. She hung her head over the rail expecting the worst. But it was a false alarm.

'It's best to keep walking,' said Annette who put her arms around Sandra's waist to help steady her. 'Let's go towards the middle of the ship,' she suggested 'It won't be so bad there.'

Sandra followed, inching her way along the rails. She looked down at the choppy sea and felt dizzy.

'Take some deep breaths,' advised Annette.

Gripping the rails with both hands, Sandra steadied herself and took a long deep breath. The fresh sea air filled her lungs to capacity and she immediately felt a clearing of her head. After a few more breaths her legs felt a bit more steady.

'What part of England you going to?' Annette inquired.

'London,' Sandra answered.

'I goin' to Birmingham. My mother send for me.'

'Your father still in Trinidad?'

'No, he went to London first. By the time my mother get to join him, he done take up with a white woman.'

Sandra was startled by Annette's frankness. 'Oh, I sorry to hear about that,' she feebly offered, not quite sure how to respond.

Annette laughed. 'I never used to see much of him even when he was in Trinidad, so I ain't miss him.'

'I don't see my father for six years now,' said Sandra as a gesture of sympathy and by way of an exchange of confidences.

'I doubt if I'll ever see my father again.' Annette spoke with indifference.

Sandra was shocked and said nothing. She was glad when Annette changed the subject.

'Let me show you some more of the ship.'

Sandra followed Annette to the stairs that led below deck. She now moved with a new confidence.

They descended narrow staircases, past their cabin and further down into the bowels of the ship. From time to time they passed members of the ship's officers and crew. Annette exchanged greetings with them as if they were old friends.

'Do you want to see the engine room?' she asked in a hushed conspiratorial tone.

'Yes,' answered Sandra, marvelling at her audacity. 'Are we allowed though?'

'Depends,' said Annette without offering any further explanation.

Sandra followed meekly down and down. The noise and heat increased dramatically as they came to the entrance of the engine room. Annette hovered at the entrance as if waiting to be noticed and invited in. Before long one of the engineers glanced up and noticed them.

'What is Annette up to now?' he enquired in a friendly fashion.

'I just brought my friend to see the engine,' she said.

'You're lucky, the skipper is on the bridge and we're not too busy now so you can have a quick look.'

Virtually all the working parts of the massive turbine engine were hidden behind metal casing. Sandra was a bit disappointed as she had expected to see a rather large version of Mr Mullings' Dodge engine.

Unable to bear the heat and noise, they soon fled to the main deck, where the air seemed fresher than before.

Before long it was time for tea, and Annette led Sandra to the large dining room where they joined a long queue. For a moment Sandra was tempted to eat something, but suddenly became aware again of the movement of the ship. She gave Annette her share.

As the evening closed in they noticed the distant outline of land to the port side of the ship and dashed over to the rails for a closer look.

'That must be Cuba,' said Annette.

Sandra saw in the distance the misty outline of land that rose out of the sea and was tinted by the crimson of the sunset.

'Cuba!' she said with a hint of wonder in her voice.

From the time she was a small child she had heard grown-ups speak about Cuba. Though Cuba was only ninety miles from Jamaica, and successive generations of Jamaicans had travelled there to seek work, Cuba remained a land of mystery.

'You can see Cuba on a clear day,' the old folk used to say. Sandra remembered how early one morning before Granny was awake, she and Leroy got out of bed and climbed the breadfruit tree at the back of their yard, ascending as high as they dared in order to get a glimpse of Cuba. For a long time they stared into the horizon, but they never saw even the faintest hint of land. To make matters worse, Granny punished them for climbing the breadfruit tree, which she considered too big for them to climb safely.

Sandra and Annette walked back to the other side of the boat, and watched in silence as Cuba slid out of sight in the fading light. It was nearing dinner time so they went back to their cabin to change.

Sandra lay on her bed exhausted. Annette shook her a few times. 'You'll miss dinner.'

'I don't want dinner.'

'You'd better get changed then or you'll fall asleep in your clothes. I'll go on alone. See you later,' said Annette.

Sandra got up and drowsily opened her case in search of her pyjamas. There at the top of the suitcase lay Lizzie!

'Thank you, Granny,' she said softly.

She took Lizzie to bed with her but she hid her under the covers and fell asleep cuddling her.

9 'You have sapadillas?'

When Sandra woke she expected to hear Granny's or Leroy's voice, but in the bunk above she heard the rhythmic breathing of Annette and remembered where she was. She still couldn't believe that she was on the high seas on her way to England.

Her bunk swayed to the ship's motion which now seemed altogether more friendly. She closed her eyes and imagined that she was being rocked in a cradle to a familiar lullaby. She had never been on holiday away from home but this was how she imagined it would feel; the day spread out before her like the open pages of an adventure book.

She wondered what new part of the ship Annette would show her today. She was tempted to wake Annette. But she didn't have to. A knock on the door woke her.

'Come in,' said Annette drowsily.

It was the stewardess who enquired after Sandra. 'How are you? Annette told me you didn't want dinner.'

'I'm fine now,' said Sandra with a genuine smile.

'Well, I hope you will eat some breakfast this morning.'

'I'll try.'

'Good, that's what I like to hear.'

In the dining room Sandra resolved to eat some breakfast, if only to please the stewardess. For the first time she found herself in the same room with people from other Caribbean islands, which till now were little more than place names and drawings in her geography book.

The food was awful.

After breakfast they headed up to the main deck. The sun was already shining brightly in the sky. Sandra went on ahead of

Annette up to the rails. She looked down at the sea and was astonished. As far as the eye could see stretched a carpet of brownish yellow seaweed, extending on either side of the ship in long regular lines.

She knew that they were in the vicinity of Bermuda and she recalled the ghoulish stories she had once read in the *Gleaner* of the Bermuda Triangle: stories of sailing ships found abandoned, their crew never to be heard of again; stories of ships that had mysteriously disappeared without trace; stories of giant sea monsters that had risen from the water and devoured whole ships.

She shuddered. She imagined that the ship would be imprisoned in the morass of weed and that they would be trapped for ever and she would never get to England and never see her mother and father again.

'We are now passing through the Sargasso Sea,' said Annette with the air of a tour guide.

There she goes again, thought Sandra, a little irritated. Miss Know-all Annette.

'I know,' she lied. Geography was not one of her strong subjects.

'You can always tell the Sargasso Sea by the amount of seaweed about.'

Listen to her, thought Sandra, biting her lips to keep her mouth shut.

'It really frightened Columbus on his first voyage. They thought they were going to get stuck,' continued Annette. 'Soon we will be in the Atlantic Ocean.'

'Columbus crossed the Atlantic in 1492,' countered Sandra. She wasn't about to let Annette assume total command.

'The *Pinta*, the *Nina* and the *Santa Maria*,' said Annette, naming the ships that made up Columbus's expedition, neatly upstaging Sandra in the process. Sandra wanted to throttle her.

They stood quietly on the bridge staring out at the horizon. Sandra racked her brain for more facts and figures about Columbus.

'Columbus came on the trade winds,' she blurted out, suddenly

50

recalling another fact from her half-forgotten history books. By some strange freak of nature a constant westerly wind blew from Europe to the Caribbean and another further north blew from the Caribbean back to Europe. It was as if nature had conspired to link these continents by defined sea lanes with backing winds and currents to ease the outward and homeward passage of ships.

'The world is really round,' pronounced Annette, as if she were supplying the final proof to some long-disputed hypothesis.

Sandra suddenly remembered Ma Becky's mangoes. Perhaps it was their round shape which made her think of them.

'Would you like a mango?' she offered.

'A real mango?' responded Annette with wide eyes.

'No, from a tin.'

Annette looked disappointed.

'Of course it's a real mango, dopey,' teased Sandra who was now glad to be in the driving seat.

They hurried to the cabin. Sandra rummaged through her food box and produced two of Ma Becky's golden ripe mangoes. As they ate them, they compared the different types of mangoes in Jamaica and Trinidad.

'You have sapadillas in Jamaica?'

'Sapadillas? I never heard of a fruit by that name.'

'It does have a smooth brown skin and shape like a guava and it brown on the inside and does have black seeds.'

'Oh, you mean naseberries,' laughed Sandra.

'Naseberries? That's what you call it?'

'Yes.'

'But it don't even look like a berry. All you should call it naseplums for it look more like a plum than a berry.'

'Anyway, whatever you call it, that is one of my favourite fruits. Next to mangoes, that is.'

'I like them too, but figs are my favourite fruit,' said Annette.

'We don't have figs in Jamaica.'

'You do!'

'No, we don't.'

'Yes, you do. I saw them being loaded on the boat at Kingston. We call them figs. You call them bananas.'

'You Trinidadians are so funny. You call bananas figs and naseberries sapadillas,' Sandra teased.

They both laughed.

'I still hungry,' said Annette licking the juice of the mangoes from her fingers.

'Me too.'

'I have some roti.'

Sandra had never heard of roti.

Annette produced a pile of flat round breads wrapped in foil from her locker.

'All you Jamaicans ain't have roti?' queried Annette with disbelief. 'We eat it with curry but my curry finish,' she explained.

'I have some akee an' saltfish. We can have it with that,' said Sandra, remembering Granny's tuck box.

'That is a new one on me, but I will give it a try.'

Sandra shared out the akee and saltfish and, following Annette's lead, broke off a bit of the roti, and used it to scoop up a mouthful of the akee and saltfish.

'Not bad,' pronounced Annette when they were finished. 'Akee and saltfish nice, but give me my curry any day.'

Five days into the voyage Sandra saw her first school of flying fish. She ran over to Annette who was seated on a deckchair. 'Come and look at the flying fish. Quick!'

'There are really some strange things in the world,' commented Annette.

No sooner had she said the words than a school of dolphins appeared as if from nowhere. They leapt in and out of the water in hot pursuit of the flying fish. The passengers gave howls of excitement every time a dolphin caught a flying fish in mid-air. After they had eaten their fill, the dolphins seemed content to follow the ship. Unable to resist an audience, they showed off by making spectacular dives in and out of the ocean and played a game of hide-and-seek with the ship.

Within a few days, Sandra and Annette became firm friends and were inseparable. One evening, mesmerised by the glorious sunset, they stayed on deck long after the other passengers had left, silently watching the last drop of colour drain away.

The ship's deck was still warm from the sun's heat, so they lay on their backs and shifted their attention to the sky which was now speckled with stars. As their bodies swayed to the ship's motion, the heavens seemed to swirl around in dizzy confusion.

'Are you glad you are going to England?' queried Sandra.

'Well, I want to see my mother,' said Annette 'But . . .' Her voice trailed off.

'But . . .?' prompted Sandra.

'But I going to miss Trinidad bad.'

'I will miss Jamaica too.'

'I miss Trinidad already an' I only leave ten days now.'

They spoke without real conviction for they were too involved in the adventure of the voyage to England.

10 The Storm

The next morning the sky was sullen and grey and unfriendly. The mirror-like sea lay quiet and still like a corpse. The freshening sea breeze had dropped and the heat was oppressive. Sandra and Annette listlessly strolled around the deck and hardly spoke.

Since they had been on deck watching the night sky, Sandra had been experiencing a strange drawing into herself. She thought it was because in less than a week she would be in England. Annette seemed to sense her mood and gave her more space than she usually did. They spent a good part of the day in the ship's small library where Sandra figured Annette had got her information on the sea.

By the afternoon a fine drizzle shrouded the ship in a veil of gloom. Sandra left Annette in the library and went down to the cabin and lay on her bunk. She wished she had stayed in the library because the cabin was quite stuffy. But she was too listless to move and wanted to be alone. She knew she was moving from one zone to the next in quick succession: from tropical to temperate, from poor to rich from black to white. It was like crossing new and uncharted rivers, for every day had brought her further away from what she knew. She felt a tightening of the muscles in the pit of her stomach. It was not painful like a stomach ache, nor queasy like when she was nervous or seasick. It was just a distant kind of numbness.

Granny would have administered some bush tea and, if that didn't work, she always carried in her head a store of handy proverbs or quotations from the Bible to illuminate any problem or lighten any load. Sandra wished she could talk to her now.

As she lay on the bunk, she was unable to discern any

movement of the sea. The calm persisted and, by evening, it had become eerie and foreboding. After dinner the captain made an announcement over the ship's loudspeaker system that the ship was temporarily changing course to avoid the centre of an approaching hurricane and advised all passengers to go to their cabins and remain there till further notice. The news snapped both Annette and Sandra out of their torpor and they became excited as they prepared for the storm.

The sea, heaped up in angry swells and white foam from the breaking waves, was blown in streaks along the direction of the wind. Suddenly the ship seemed smaller and more fragile. The bow rose and fell with each swell and, when the ship dropped over the crest of a large wave, sheets of fine salty spray were thrown into the air. The ship's metal plates, planks, beams and rivets creaked and groaned more than ever as she ploughed through the rough seas.

Once in the cabin, the girls quickly changed and got into bed and switched off the lights. They felt safe, with their heads buried under their covers like a pair of ostrichs, while the storm raged around them.

'You awake, Annette?'

'Yes.'

'You think the ship going to sink?'

'I hope not.'

'The waves must be big, for true!'

'Yes.' Annette climbed out of her bunk and went over to the porthole. She peeped out. 'Come and look, Sandra.'

Sandra made her way to the porthole, using the uprights of the berth as support. Her cheeks were almost touching Annette's as she peered out into the darkness at the raging sea. It was reassuring to feel the warmth of another body, but she wished she had stayed in her bunk.

The sea was illuminated from time to time by flashes of lightning. Angry waves as tall as government buildings rose up from the depths of the ocean and crashed about the ship. Occasionally the sky was streaked by long jagged bolts of fork lightning.

In the darkness they waited for the loud claps of thunder, but from the insulation of the cabin they could hear nothing but the beating of their hearts. The flying storm clouds broke for an instant; the light of the moon filtered through the gap and, like a powerful floodlight in a theatre, lit up the scene. All around white foam boiled madly.

The ship hurled downwards and crashed into the sea like a large brick against concrete. The girls were thrown against the floor of the ship like a pair of rag dolls. They lay in the darkness for a while, not quite sure whether they were dead or alive.

Sandra groped in the darkness for Annette. It was Annette's hand which first found hers.

'Are you OK?' Annette asked in an anxious voice.

Sandra felt bruised and battered but otherwise intact. 'I think so. What about you?'

'I'm scared.'

Sandra knew it was difficult for Annette to admit it. She crawled over to the door and turned on the light. The floor of the cabin was strewn with their belongings. Having the light on somewhat lessened the terror. They staggered back into bed and battened themselves down under their covers to ride out the rest of the storm.

The swirling ocean settled down into long rolling waves. The ship went into a rolling motion.

The girls' fear was replaced by seasickness.

'I feel sick,' said Sandra.

'Me too.'

But to get to the toilet meant leaving the cabin and venturing down the passage outside. They lay in bed and hoped that their stomachs would settle. All they could hear was the faint pelting of rain against the porthole. It had a soothing effect – like the sound of the rain on a zinc roof and reminded Sandra of home.

But still the feeling of nausea persisted. (How she wished that Granny was in the next room.) Then she remembered Granny's brown paper. She clambered out of the bunk and fetched it from her locker. She tore the paper into two halves and handed one to Annette.

'Try this.'

'What's this all about?' muttered Annette.

'Just try it. It's for seasickness,' said Sandra.

Annette watched with disbelief as Sandra placed the brown paper under her nighty and hopped back into bed. Annette did the same.

Sandra wasn't quite sure whether it was the brown paper or the stabilising of the ship, but their stomachs settled and they both slept like logs for the rest of the night.

As they lay in their bunks the next morning Sandra was about to bounce out of bed when she realised that something was wrong. She felt a moistness between her legs. She sprang out of bed in a panic and threw the covers up.

'Annette, Annette, I'm bleeding. I'm dying!'

Annette jumped down from the top bunk and looked for herself. She then started to laugh uncontrollably. 'You're having your period. Don't you know about that?'

Sandra knew about it in some vague sort of way but, now that it had happened to her, it still took her by surprise and struck fear into her heart.

'It's OK,' said Annette. 'I know what you need.'

Sandra knew that she was crossing another river and that Granny had sent her ahead of Leroy so that her mother could help her to negotiate a safe path.

For days afterwards, the passengers spoke of nothing but the storm. Rain squalls increasingly ambushed them and sudden winds sent light spray over the weather rail. It grew colder in the North Atlantic as they neared England. Sandra and Annette had to fish their jumpers from their suitcases. It was the first time Sandra had worn a jumper and she wore it with a certain self-conscious pride.

It was a calm silver-grey morning when the girls stood on the main deck and got their first glimpse of land through the haze of fog that enveloped the English Channel.

'I told you I would see England first!' boasted Annette, claiming to win their bet.

But they soon discovered it wasn't England, but the Isle of Wight. And by the time the faint outline of Southampton emerged from the mist there was no element of surprise and they decided on a friendly draw.

Bit by bit the faint outline of Southampton defined itself. Oil refineries and massive industrial buildings; church steeples and the domed tops of buildings, then finally rows and rows of white terraced houses.

The harbour was dotted with trawlers and yachts and motor boats of all shapes and sizes. Sandra was struck by the sheer size of the docks. Scores of tall cranes hovered above large merchant vessels and the dockside buzzed with activity.

When the ship entered the harbour, two tugboats drew alongside and were secured to the ship by thick cables. They slowly guided the ship to its resting place by the dockside.

Sandra and Annette had their hand luggage sorted out, and were amongst the first to be taken by the purser to form a line to present themselves, one by one, to the immigration officer.

Sandra was suddenly aware of the sea of white faces around her. Annette would soon disappear through the barrier in front of her and be swept away by her family. Sandra realised how much she had relied on Annette during the journey and felt tears well up in her now that it was time to say goodbye to her.

'Bye, Sandra.'

'Bye, Annette.'

There was nothing else to say. She reproached herself for getting so close to Annette, for now she knew that friendships brought tearful separation. She thought of Lorna.

Annette wasn't long at the immigration desk, and as she crossed the barrier she turned and gave Sandra a cheerful goodbye wave.

Then it was Sandra's turn. She was filled with trepidation as the officer flicked through her passport and immigration documents. She had heard sad stories, recounted with bitterness, of people who had saved up and travelled all the way to England only to be turned back by immigration officers because their papers were judged not to be in order. But she needn't have worried. The immigration officer examined her passport, stamped it and motioned her towards the barrier.

Sandra passed through the barrier. She was on English soil and it took a while to sink in, and Sandra just stood there, motionless. The stewardess nudged her in the direction of a crowd of people waiting about twenty metres away. 'Your family are over there.'

At last I will see Dadda, she thought, but as soon as the thought passed through her mind she was seized with a sudden and overwhelming panic. She didn't know what to look for.

The idea of being met by strangers in a strange land filled her with dread.

PART THREE – ENGLAND

11 The Meeting

Sandra scanned the horizon of faces, but they all seemed the same: faces with fixed smiles, waiting for friends or relatives to come into view. What if they weren't there? Suppose they were mistaken about the time of the ship's arrival? She felt indescribably lonely.

Then suddenly her parents seemed to materialise out of thin air. Her mother and father were barely recognisable in their heavy winter coats and the twins bore no resemblance to the photographs of the two tots that stood on Granny's dressing table. They all four presented a picture of a compact family unit, complete and self-contained. She felt like an outsider meeting a strange family for the first time and wasn't at all sure what to do.

Something of her bewilderment must have been communicated to them for their greetings were restrained and tentative. Her mother kissed her lightly on the cheek with a faint 'hello'. Her attention was divided between Sandra and the twins who clutched her legs from a mixture, it seemed, of bashfulness and possessiveness.

She could see from her father's expression that he was still carrying around a mental picture of her the way she was when he left Jamaica. 'What a way you turn a big girl on me!' he teased, as if she had grown up just to spite him. He stood back for a moment appraising her. A broad grin slowly reshaped his face as if what he saw met with his approval.

For years Sandra had imagined the moment when she would see her father again; how she would run wildly towards him and throw her arms around his neck with shrieks of delight and how he would in turn hug and kiss her and twirl her round and round till she was giddy with happiness.

But now, to her surprise, standing facing her father, she found she could not move or speak.

Her father kissed her on her cheek and put an arm round her. Her chest tightened and, instead of the laughter and joy she had imagined, she found herself fighting back the tears.

They were not the tears of sadness that she had cried as she watched the receding figures of Granny and Leroy, or the tears of happiness she had shed when she first received Lizzie. These were nameless tears; the kind of inconsiderate, embarrassing tears that sprang up unannounced and caught you unawares. She was determined not to give way to them for though the occasion was not the joyful one she had dreamt of, she wanted it to be light-hearted at least. She lowered her face, partly out of shyness, and partly to hide the small trickle of tears that had breached her defences and played around the corners of her eyes.

'Let me introduce you to your brother Wayne, and your sister Jean,' her father said.

The formality of the introduction took Sandra aback.

'Hello, Jean,' she greeted her little sister, putting out her hand to touch her, to make some contact. But Jean pulled away and hid her face in the folds of her mother's dress.

Sandra knew it was foolish to feel hurt by the action of a four-year-old child but she couldn't help it. She didn't want to risk the same response from Wayne, so she nodded meekly in his direction. She felt in that instant that she had lost her mother and father to two strange children and her feeling of being a stranger in a strange land with a stranger family was complete.

The chill of the November day forced them to seek the warmth of the train. Coldness wrapped itself round Sandra and seeped into her very bones. She secretly smiled when she remembered how naive she was to think that placing her hand on a block of ice would have prepared her for this kind of cold.

It shocked Sandra to see white men wheeling trolleys with luggage or emptying rubbish containers or sweeping the platform. She had always associated white people with office jobs requiring collar and tie and clean hands because, in Jamaica, she had never seen a white bus driver or carpenter, let alone a cane cutter or market higgler.

And now as the train picked up speed and entered open country she was glad to be able to look at it because her shyness in the presence of her family persisted. The land seemed cold and indifferent like the face of the immigration officer. In every direction lay neatly parcelled plots of rolling fields of differing shades of green. Each field was bordered by hedgerows of shrubs or trees, which gave the land the appearance of the assembled pieces of a jigsaw puzzle that were measured, portioned off and sealed off from trespassers.

She was surprised to see so few farm animals, apart from a few grazing sheep and a field with two horses. They travelled for quite a while before Sandra saw any sign of human life in the form of a farmer driving a tractor across a field.

'How is Mamma and Leroy?' her father asked at length.

'They're fine,' she answered, thinking it odd that anyone should refer to Granny as 'Mamma'. 'What about your Uncle Bertie?'

'He's fine too.' She could think of nothing more to say, for try as she might she could not overcome the awkwardness that tied her tongue.

'And Miss Simpson, how is she? Last time Granny write she say she sick.'

'She's OK now,' answered Sandra, anxious not to repeat the word 'fine' for the umpteenth time.

They were silent for a while. Her mother started the ball rolling again. 'The clothes we send fit all right?'

'Yes, Mamma.' She knew better than to mention the oversize coat.

Sandra wanted to describe shopping with Granny but her tongue was still weighed down with shyness.

Her father took up the challenge. 'What about old man Goldsmith? He still alive?'

'Yes, he's still alive.'

'What about Cutty?'

'Cutty?' Sandra queried.

'Yes, you know, the fellow with the bend foot. Always dancing masquerade at Christmas time?'

Sandra smiled. She was stumped by that one and the generation gap was beginning to tell.

'Yes, the one that dance up and down wearing the horse head. Used to frighten the life out us when we was little!'

'I don't know about him, Dadda.'

'Must be dead and gone by now,' concluded her father, convinced at last that something had changed in the town since he'd left. 'Mas' Ken still have his rum shop?'

'Yes, and he build a restaurant upstairs.'

Her father paused for a while as if going through an inventory of half-forgotten names in his mind. Then his face brightened with a smile. 'What about Ma Becky? She still as miserable as ever?'

Sandra smiled to herself. She was tempted to tell her father that Ma Becky had given her some mangoes before she left, but it wouldn't make much sense to him unless she told the full story. It all seemed too much to tell so she just nodded with a faint smile.

'When I was a boy, Ma Becky ketch me thiefing her mangoes so much time I los' count,' her father laughed.

So there was a history to that mango tree! Two generations of the James family had raided her mangoes! Sandra smiled in spite of herself.

Her father was silent for a while as if trying to figure some new strategy to get Sandra to talk and make the conversation less one-sided.

Then Sandra remembered the letter. 'Leroy send a letter with me,' she volunteered.

She was acutely aware that her parents eyed her with a mixture of amusement and mild astonishment as she rummaged in her handbag for the letter. She knew that they hadn't expected her to be so grown up. She felt a certain pride in her role as courier.

Her mother read the letter, her lips silently mouthing the words as her eyes moved across the page.

It took Sandra a while to figure out what was different about her father. At first she had put it down to his strange clothes. Suddenly she realised it was his moustache, which was so faint that it was little more than a thin line traced with a pen.

Finally her mother finished the letter and handed it to him.

'Let me see your passport picture,' asked her mother. She studied the picture for a while. 'You turn a big girl now,' she said, looking at the photograph as if she found it easier to speak to the picture of Sandra than directly to her. 'It's a nice picture. Who tek it?'

'A photographer in Ocho Rios.'

'Your grandmother took you to Ocho Rios?'

'No, me and Leroy took the bus by ourselves.'

'Leroy must be a big man now.'

'Leroy almost as tall as Dadda,' said Sandra with pride. Her mother forced a rueful smile.

'Let me see!' said Wayne, reaching for the passport.

'No, let me see!' screamed Jean, snatching the passport from Wayne.

'I had it first,' said Wayne, snatching it back.

'Don't tear Sandra's passport,' admonished their mother. 'You can both look at it at the same time.'

'Who is it, Mum?' asked Wayne, peering at the photograph.

'That's Sandra, silly,' said his mum. 'Your sister! See, she's sitting right in front of you.'

Wayne and Jean looked at the photograph and then at Sandra and then at the photograph again as if trying to make some connection between the photograph and their strange sister sitting opposite them. They started to giggle.

'Let your father see the picture,' said her mother, passing the passport to him. He looked at the picture wistfully. 'Only Leroy left to come up now.' He spoke with more resignation than pride.

Her mother seemed weighted down by the demands of the two small children, who still clung to her, and who viewed Sandra through suspicious, uncomprehending eyes. Presently they fell asleep and her mother dozed off too.

For the twenty minutes or so before they pulled into Waterloo Station, Sandra had her dad all to herself. She relaxed somewhat as she told him more and more about Leroy and Granny and the other people in the village. He laughed uproariously when she told him about Ma Becky and the mangoes.

As they reached the outskirts of London, Sandra was amazed by the sight of rows upon rows of joined-up houses with their small rectangular back gardens bordering the railway line. At school Sandra had read about cities where people lived close together, but this was her first real glimpse of it.

She thought of Granny and wondered how she would have managed with such a small backyard. Where would she have put her chickens and ducks and where would she have planted her bush for tea and her banana trees and her vegetable patch? As the train got nearer and nearer to the heart of the city, the buildings got more clustered and reached higher into the sky. Sandra felt dwarfed.

They at last got off the train and stood on the platform as her father sought out a porter to carry the luggage. Sandra looked around in amazement. The station was like a massive cathedral whose domed glass roof echoed the bustle below of the coming and going of trains and the opening and slamming of their doors.

They followed the porter to the street. A light drizzle started to fall and shrouded everything in a dull grey uniform. Her father hailed a black taxi. As the taxi pulled out of the station and joined the busy central London traffic, Sandra felt quite overwhelmed by the sheer volume of traffic and the density of the crowds that rushed about in every direction. The buildings, ancient and modern, large and small, seemed to jostle for limited space. Before long she got her first sight of the famous red double-decker buses.

'This is Trafalgar Square, and that's Nelson's Column,' said her father, sticking his hand out of the window and pointing up to the sky at the lone figure of Nelson perched at the top of the towering column.

As he pulled the window down, a gust of cold air blew into the taxi. Sandra shivered and pulled her overcoat tightly around her. She remembered the photo of her father with three other men, taken in front of one of the lions. The photograph must have been taken on a summer's day for her father and his friends were all dressed in open-neck shirts. They had stood, optimistic and triumphant, in front of the lion as if they had slain it on some imaginary safari.

'That's where you took the picture, Dadda,' she reminded him.

'Yes, that was a long time ago.' His eyes glazed over for a brief moment then a shadow crossed his face.

'Buckingham Palace is along that road,' he said, pointing in the direction of a large stone gateway. Then on an impulse he said to the taxi driver, 'Take us past Buckingham Palace.'

The driver veered to the left and drove through the gateway and on to a wide tree-lined avenue paved with red asphalt and skirted by an open park to the left, and a row of stately cream-coloured buildings on the right. After a few hundred metres Buckingham Palace came into view. It was set back from the road and was surrounded by high railings.

'It's got six hundred rooms,' her father said.

In spite of all those rooms, Sandra was a bit disappointed with Buckingham Palace.

They headed towards home, passing Hyde Park and up towards Marble Arch. 'That's Speakers' Corner over there,' he said. 'I used to go down there on a Sunday morning to listen to people speak.' He chuckled as if he was reliving some treasured moment. 'But I don't have time for that sort of thing no more,' he added. 'Mind you, those fellows can speak, you know! And they can say any damn thing they like and nobody going to tell them they can't say it. Free speech! That's what they call it. A few West Indian fellows used to speak there every Sunday – probably still do, for all I know. They use to have us in stitches. And you have a lot of cranks there too, I can tell you!'

When the taxi had gone a little distance up the Edgware Road, it turned left into the Harrow Road and sped towards north-west London. The buildings got smaller and more ordinary as the journey progressed and soon her father seemed to have run out of interesting landmarks to point out.

At last the taxi pulled up in front of a modest red-bricked terrace house.

'We're home,' announced her father with forced cheerfulness.

12 Home

Her father fidgeted with a number of keys before finding the right one. It was dark inside and a musty smell clung to the walls. He switched on a bare light bulb which lit up a narrow passage and staircase. The wooden staircase squeaked noisily as they struggled up the stairs with the luggage.

They came to a door on the first-floor landing. Keys jingled again as he opened the front door of their flat, turned on the light and lugged the suitcases to a room that led off from the passage. Her mother went through into the front room and opened the curtains to let in some natural light.

Sandra followed her father into a small bedroom. There were bunk beds in one corner and a single bed opposite. He put down the suitcases by the bed. Sandra was glad that it was away from the window, for she could feel the chill coming from behind the curtains.

'You have to share with the twins,' announced her father as he put down the suitcases. 'But only for a little while till we get a bigger place,' he added apologetically.

She was dismayed but the cold dispelled any other thought from her head. She hugged herself and shuddered.

'You feel cold, eh?' he enquired, rubbing his hands together with a degree of relish, as if he was trying to reassure her that the cold wasn't such a bad thing after all.

'I will light the fire, I don't want you freezing to death.' He laughed to reassure her that he was only joking. Sandra was grateful. There was a muffled pop as the gas ignited into a bright orange flare before settling down into a steady clear blue flame.

Sandra watched entranced, as the clear blue flames, the only reminder of the skies in Jamaica, gradually turned the base of the white grill into a cosy red glow. Then she shuddered again when she realised that it seemed to make no difference to the temperature of the room. Sandra wondered if she would ever, ever be warm again.

'The room will soon warm up,' reassured her father. 'You will soon get accustomed to the cold,' he added still smiling.

Sandra looked round the room. She felt depressed, not just because of the dull patterned wallpaper or the smallness of the room, or the fact she had to share it with virtual strangers, but because nobody had warned her that in England the grey clouds could be thick enough in the middle of the day to block out the light of the sun. Nobody had told her that curtains would be drawn against the cold of the day, and that the main source of light would be from an electric bulb, and the only real heat from some man-made contraption.

Sandra didn't complain for Granny had taught her to always make the best of whatever situation you find yourself in. She sat on the bed and folded her arms in a hugging motion, moving her arms up and down and rubbing herself in an attempt to stimulate her circulation.

Her father saw her misery and left the room. Sandra thought he was giving her a chance to acclimatise herself to her new surroundings, but he shortly returned with a paraffin heater which he quickly lit. Sandra suddenly noticed the neat bunch of flowers on the bedside table. This cheered her up as she guessed it was her mother's quiet gesture of welcome. That was her mother's way for, like Granny, she had never been one for hugs and kisses.

Once the twins were on their home territory they became more confident, running from room to room.

Sandra busied herself unpacking the presents that she had brought from Granny. Apart from two T-shirts for the twins with 'I love Jamaica' emblazoned on the front with a bright yellow sun and green palms in the background from Leroy and herself, all the other presents were food and mostly made by Granny. There were bottles of Solomon Gundy, pickled peppers

71

and hot pepper sauce for the grown-ups, guava jelly made with guavas from her own trees, tambrind balls, gazzada cakes, coconut cakes and all manner of candied fruits.

The twins showed an immediate interest in the candies and Sandra had her first breakthrough when, after an initial moment's hesitation, they each accepted a coconut cake. They inspected the unfamiliar object with suspicion before tentatively taking a taste.

'Ughhhhhhhh!' they exclaimed with disgust.

What strange children, Sandra thought, who didn't like Granny's coconut cakes.

'These children only like English food,' her father said with mock despair. 'Give them fish an' chips an' they happy.'

'With your father around they won't go to waste,' said her mother with what Sandra detected to be the first hint of cheer in her voice. That was the cue for her father to tuck into the coconut cakes with gusto.

'It's years now since I eat coconut cakes,' he said, relishing them it seemed more from nostalgia than for their taste.

Sandra continued with her unpacking when she came across Lizzie, neatly packed amongst her clothes. She placed Lizzie on the bed.

'That's a big doll!' said Wayne.

'It's the biggest doll ever!' said Jean.

They came over and examined Lizzie with curiosity. Before long they had taken over Lizzie and were playing with her on the bunk bed. Sandra fought back feelings of possessiveness. At least she was able to make up for the disappointment with the sweets.

Sandra looked around the rest of the flat. It was strangely familiar in a library-book sort of way. The small window with its drawn curtains, the wallpaper, the light bulb, closed around her. She felt claustrophobic. After two weeks holed up aboard ship all she wanted to do was to fling off her jumper and her shoes and to run free as if she were in Granny's backyard.

Later her mum fixed a meal which they ate at a dining table in the kitchen. There were no yams or sweet potatoes or fried plantains yet it was still unmistakably West Indian in flavour. The twins were served what her mother called fish fingers and beans

72

and potatoes. She wondered when she would get her first taste of English food.

Before long the excitement of the day began to take its toll and Sandra wilted visibly.

'You better get some sleep.' Her mother sounded as if she was giving an order and not just advice. She followed Sandra into the room. 'Your father light two fires for you?'

'Yes . . .'

'You lucky,' her mother said dolefully. 'Anyway it's warm enough now.' She turned off the paraffin heater. Sandra wished she had left it on.

'It not good to sleep with the heater on,' she added as if she had read Sandra's thoughts. 'You will wake up in the morning with a headache.'

She produced a pair of woollen pyjamas. Sandra was impressed by their thickness. She clutched the pyjamas to her body, waiting for her mother to leave the room so that she could change in privacy but her mother hovered. How strange it was to be embarrassed to undress in front of your own mother, she thought, as she fidgeted with her dress to delay changing. Finally her mother tired of waiting and retired to the kitchen.

Sandra slid under the covers and felt as if she was lying on a slab of ice. Her body heat soon transferred to the middle of the bed and she curled up her legs to avoid the icy wastes below. Bit by bit she straightened her legs, slowly extending her empire. At last she bravely thrust out both legs to their full length, only to swiftly pull them back when her feet came into contact with the cold sheets.

She remained in a foetal position and closed her eyes, waiting for sleep to overtake her. Family noises and the sound of the TV drifted in from the front room which made her wish that she had stayed up to get her first view of TV. From the flat above she heard the muted sound of footsteps and from below the rattling of kitchen utensils. There were strangers living above her and below her in the same house! This city living would take some getting used to. Outside, she heard the sounds of the occasional swish-swishing of tyres on wet asphalt as cars drove up and down the road, and beyond, the faint murmur of a city whose immensity was beyond her imagination.

Yet compared to Jamaica the night was quiet and restrained. Sandra thought of Granny and Leroy on the other side of the world. What were they doing now? What time was it in Jamaica anyway? She felt cold again and wished that she had Granny to snuggle up against as she used to do for a while after her mum had left for England. Then she had a thought. She slipped quietly out of bed and went over to the twins' bunks and retrieved Lizzie from the bottom one.

She returned to bed with Lizzie snuggled up beside her and fell asleep with the words on her lips: 'I want to go home. I want to go home.'

13 'When is Leroy coming up, Mamma?'

Sandra had no idea for how long she slept. The curtains were drawn and the room was semi-dark. There was no sign of the twins. Lizzie was propped up against a pillow on the bottom bunk. The little devils, she thought, they must have kidnapped her while she slept.

The gas fire had been lit. The room was warm but the bed was so cosy that she didn't want to get up. It was the first time since encountering the cold in the mid-Atlantic that she had really felt warm. She heard her mother pottering around in the kitchen. She had taken the day off work to help Sandra settle. Her father, who was working nights, was probably asleep.

Sandra glanced at her watch. It was 11 a.m. She felt guilty lying in bed while her mother was doing the household chores. Granny would have scolded her if she could see her now, relaxing while her mother was busy. She got up and made her bed. She smiled when she remembered how cross Granny would be if she didn't make up her bed. 'The same way you leave your bed in the mornings is the same way you going have to lie in it come night-time!'

After she had dressed and freshened herself up she went to the kitchen.

'Morning, Mamma.'

'Good morning, Sandra. You had a good night's sleep?'

'Yes.'

'You ready for breakfast?'

Sandra nodded.

'Try some baked beans on toast,' coaxed her mother.

She tried a mouthful. 'Hmmmm,' she said approvingly.

Her mother smiled and popped another slice of bread in the toaster. How easy it was! Just to put the sliced bread in the toaster and watch it pop up all brown and ready to be smeared with lashings of butter.

Later her mother helped Sandra finish unpacking and came across a half-empty packet of sanitary pads. Sandra felt as if some guilty secret had been uncovered.

'How long you been using these?' her mum asked.

'That's the first pack.'

'You bought it before you left, just in case?'

Sandra knew her mother was probing. 'Granny bought them for me.'

'Oh,' said her mother, as if she were relieved that her daughter hadn't had to fend for herself without her mother. Sandra didn't have the heart to tell her about her traumas on the boat and about Annette.

'We have to buy you some clothes for the winter,' her mother said without enthusiasm. 'Only God knows where we will get the money from,' she added as an afterthought to no one in particular.

Sandra felt a stab of guilt. Granny was always telling her and Leroy about the sacrifices that their mother and father made for them. She was grateful but still resented her mother making her feel guilty about it. It wasn't her fault that they had decided to come to live in this wretched cold country!

She tried to remind herself that she was now at home but her heart told her that Granny was her mother and her home was in Jamaica with her. After they had finished unpacking they relaxed in the kitchen and chatted while her mother fixed a light lunch. As they ate, she asked Sandra about friends and family she had left in Jamaica.

No sooner was lunch finished than her mother started to prepare the evening meal. 'I'd better do it now as I have to fetch the twins later and they take up so much of my time,' she explained.

Sandra peeled potatoes and carrots. Afterwards she peeled the onions which made her eyes smart and water.

76

'I hope Leroy behaving himself in Jamaica.'

'Oh, yes . . .'

'An' not giving your grandmother any trouble.'

'No, Mamma,' said Sandra truthfully.

'He have any girlfriends?'

'Not really . . .'

'What you mean, not really. He either have girlfriends or he don't.'

'What I mean is that he don't have any special girlfriends.'

'You mean he have a whole heap of girlfriends, eh?'

'Not really, Mamma . . .'

'What you mean then, girl? It must either be one thing or the other.'

'What I mean is that a lot of girls like him but he don't bother with any one in particular. He is just nice to all of them alike.'

'Well, I'm glad to hear. What he doing with girlfriends at his age anyway, eh? When children get to that age they should be worrying about their school books and nothing else.'

Sandra nodded mechanically for she had no strong feelings on the matter, and she suspected that the little lecture was really for her benefit.

She got up and went to the window and looked out. Everything outside looked grubby and depressing in the grey half-light. The little rectangle of grass was barely big enough to turn around in. There was a tree in the middle of the garden with two tiny forlorn apples clinging to its leafless branches and to the rear stood a small shed. A rusty garden rake lay on the ground and was nearly hidden by coarse tufts of grass growing around it. Not very inviting, so she didn't mind if they didn't have the use of it.

Inside, the kitchen was lit up by a bare electric light which threw a harsh arc of light across the ceiling which was stained brown by smoke and oil from years of cooking.

Sandra turned and faced her mother. She was sitting directly under the light and dark shadows ringed her eyes.

'When is Leroy coming up, Mamma?'

Her mother was silent for a while. 'God alone knows.'

Sandra felt that she had chosen the wrong moment to raise the subject.

'We can't send for Leroy till we have the money for the passage and till we have a bigger place. We couldn't expect him to sleep in the front room. It wouldn't be fair on him or the rest of you children as you have to have a room to relax in.'

Sandra felt depressed. She wondered whether she would ever see Leroy again.

14 'She's not my sister'

'It's my room.'

Mum intervened. 'You have to share the room with your sister now.'

'She's not my sister!'

'She's not my sister,' echoed Wayne like a little parrot.

'Of course she is you sister. How many times do I have to explain to you that Sandra is your older sister and that she was born in Jamaica long before either of you.'

'We were born in Jamaica too,' said Wayne.

'You were both born in London,' explained Mum patiently.

'No, I was born in Jamaica.'

'Me too,' insisted Jean, pouting her mouth as large tears rolled down her cheeks.

Mum gave up. 'OK, OK. You were all born in Jamaica.'

That seemed to satisfy the twins and they cheered up.

Sandra left them and headed for the front room where she heard the sound of the TV.

'Hello, Dadda,' she said.

'Hi, Sandra.' He glanced at her from behind a newspaper. On the screen was horse-racing. Sandra wondered how her father was watching TV and reading at the same time.

She sat on the settee and gaped at the black and white screen. The horses were taking a long time to line up to start the racing while the commentators prattled on about the odds. It was boring. She wondered why her father bothered to watch.

As soon as the race started her father became quite animated. 'Come on, boy, come on, boy!' he shouted, whipping some imaginary horse he was riding.

'Stupid horse!' he hissed at the end of the race, angrily discarding the newspaper. Sandra wondered why he got so upset.

'Are you ready, Sandra?' her mother called from the passage.

'Yes, Mamma.'

'She called you Mamma,' said Wayne. Jean giggled.

'Her name is Mum, not Mamma,' said Wayne as if Sandra had made a very silly mistake indeed.

'I can call her Mamma if I like,' insisted Sandra.

'She accustom to call me Mamma from she little,' said her mum. 'Come, Sandra, let's go.'

It was Saturday and they were going shopping. Sandra skipped out on to the pavement ahead of her mother. She still felt cold, but her excitement at the prospect of venturing out into the streets of London had made the cold bearable. Her overcoat seemed to fit better over a jumper. She felt a kind of exhilaration sweep through her that made her rub her hands together as if she relished the cold, just like her father.

As she breathed, clouds of hoary frost bellowed from her nostrils and mouth, and she amused herself for a while by smoking an imaginary cigarette. Presently her mother emerged from the house and Sandra immediately quit her 'smoking' in case her mother might think she indulged in the real thing.

As she walked down the High Street with her mother, she wanted to keep her smile near the surface and at the ready just as Granny would have liked. 'Laugh and the whole world laughs with you, weep and you weep alone' was one of Granny's favourite proverbs.

But nobody laughed. Nobody smiled. Nobody even seemed to notice them. How strange Sandra thought. Not so much a 'howdy' or 'good morning'. Not even a nod. What would Granny have thought of this place London which displayed only a sea of silent white faces with glazed eyes that didn't see you?

Sandra experienced the strange sensation that she and her mother were somehow invisible. To see and not to be seen, to be there and not to be there. She felt the smile that she had held near the surface slowly melt away.

They entered a large department store and made their way to

the school-uniform section on the first floor. A brisk, efficient woman helped them select two pleated grey skirts, a blue and green striped tie and several white shirts and pairs of knee-length grey socks. Sandra tried to imagine what she would look like when they were on, and thought it would make a nice change from the navy blue school uniforms that she had worn in Jamaica.

On their way home they stopped at a large supermarket to do their weekend shopping. Sandra wheeled the trolley behind her mother, amazed as they made their way between shelves laden with canned and packaged food. At the greengrocer's, Sandra and her mother waited in a queue to be served. In Jamaica fruits and vegetables were bought in the market and Sandra had never seen the market crowded enough to make queueing necessary.

Here the orderliness of the queue was in marked contrast to the hustle and bustle of the market back home. A light drizzle had started yet nobody took cover. Apart from one or two people in the queue who opened umbrellas, everybody stoically accepted the miserable conditions and patiently waited their turn.

Sandra stuffed her gloved hands in her pockets to keep them warm but there wasn't much she could do about the soles of her feet which she could swear were turning to blocks of ice.

Eventually it was their turn to be served. The greengrocer, a jolly red-haired man with a walrus moustache, was the first friendly stranger Sandra had met. Sandra held the shopping bag open as her mother packed it.

'You got a new assistant, I see,' he said to her mother, nodding in the direction of Sandra.

'Is my daughter!' said her mother with a touch of pride.

'Been hiding her, 'ave you? I ain't seen her before.'

'She just come up from Jamaica.'

'Fancy leaving all that lovely sunshine?' said the greengrocer, genuinely puzzled. Sandra knew the answer only too well and knew instinctively that he could never really understand why people have to pack up and leave their lovely warm country for a strange cold land. She was glad however for his friendliness and managed a weak smile in return.

It had taken an effort for her to smile, and it suddenly occurred to her that she had been so busy holding her smile in check that her cheeks were beginning to hurt.

'That will be two pounds, eight shillings and sixpence, luv,' said the greengrocer who had been keeping a tally of the cost as he went along, writing the cost of each item down on a brown paper bag.

Straightaway her mother opened her purse and handed over a five-pound note.

That was another surprise for Sandra. There was no bargaining over prices! What a funny country!

Back home, Granny would have had so much fun haggling over the prices. At the end of one of these haggling sessions, the market woman would give Granny an extra mango or a tomato as a sweetener or 'brawta' as they called it, and there would be smiles all around.

Sandra soon discovered that in England fish too was sold in a shop all by itself. What was more, they scaled and cleaned the fish for you. And chopped the head off too. Granny would have been horrified, for she boiled the head to extract every last ounce of flavour for the gravy or to make fish soup.

Sandra was even more astonished when her mother took her into a sweet shop. There were more kinds of sweets than she imagined existed. Her mother bought some chocolate for the twins. 'What you want, Sandra?' she asked.

Confronted with such a novel array of sweets and chocolates, she didn't know what to ask for. 'I'll have some paradise plums.'

'Paradise plums!' laughed her mother. 'You won't find those in England.'

Sandra thought of asking for mint balls but held her tongue in case they didn't make them in England either. Her mum came to the rescue. 'Try a Mars Bar.'

'OK,' said Sandra, when what she really wanted to say was, 'What's that?' But anything, however trivial, that made her feel like an outsider was to be avoided. It would give her so much pleasure to write to Granny and tell her how marvellous England was and how well she had fitted into English society and how much she was liking it. She knew that Granny would have felt proud and would have taken some of the credit for bringing her up the right way.

At length they returned home laden, carrier bags swinging from both their hands. Sandra had never seen so much food bought in one go. At home people bought their meat and fish and most of their fruits and vegetables fresh because not many people had fridges.

Sandra spent the rest of Saturday relaxing and watching television. Television opened a window on to the secrets and mysteries of English life from the warmth and safety of her own living room.

As she watched, the twins came and curled up beside her on the sofa. They lost some of their self-consciousness and became visibly more relaxed. Sandra felt herself warming to her ready-made brother and sister.

Before she went to bed that night she laid out the clothes she would wear to church the next morning. Then she remembered the hat. She only hoped that she wouldn't feel too embarrassed. Suppose girls her age didn't wear hats to church?

But she need not have worried, because Sunday morning came and went and there was not a stir in the house. The twins, who had been allowed to stay up late, slept like logs and neither her mother nor father emerged from their room. Sandra lay in bed trying to fathom Sunday morning without the ringing of church bells and without the sound of Granny's voice urging her to get out of bed.

Yes, England was full of surprises.

15 Off to School

Sandra hardly had time to catch her breath and settle in before being ushered off to school. Just my luck to arrive in England in November – smack bang in the middle of school term, she thought.

Her mother took time off work to accompany her to the school which was a fairly long bus ride away. Sandra would have to make her way back home alone, so she had to pay careful attention. Her mother had offered to come to the school to fetch her, but Sandra knew that it would be inconvenient and that money would be docked from her wages, so she persuaded her mother that she could manage.

They waited at the bus stop till at last a number 18 double-decker bus emerged on the horizon. Sandra and her mother hopped on to the open platform at the rear of the bus and took a seat downstairs. She envied those children who sat on the upper deck, even if she wasn't totally convinced that such a top-heavy bus wouldn't topple over sooner or later. She resolved to sit upstairs on her way back home.

She felt proud and grown up when her mother reached into her handbag and handed her a pair of keys. She had never travelled anywhere with keys before because in Jamaica when she and Granny went out in daytime they had never had to lock up.

'Don't worry,' said her mum, 'there will be a lot of children taking the same bus on the way back from school.'

Sandra was too worried about the school day to think that far ahead.

The first sight of the school filled her with foreboding. It was a four-storey Victorian brick building surrounded by concrete play areas. They made their way up a winding staircase, past droves of confident children charging up and down the stairs, and on to the landing which led to the school secretary's office.

'I am Mrs James,' her mother said to the secretary, a stout woman in her mid-forties. 'I came about my daughter, Sandra.'

'Ah yes, I remember,' said the secretary and took a folder out from an office file. 'I'll take you to Mr Francis, the headmaster. He's expecting you.'

Sandra and her mother trailed behind the secretary. Their footsteps echoed on the concrete passage. Presently they arrived at the headmaster's office.

After preliminary greetings he spoke to Sandra. 'Well, I hope you had a pleasant trip up.'

'Yes, sir,' Sandra answered.

'And welcome to St John's,' he continued. 'I hope that you will enjoy your stay here and work hard.'

Sandra smiled weakly and nodded.

'You are to be in 2C, Miss Claire's class, where you'll be taken shortly. I'm sure you'll make lots of friends and settle in very quickly.'

Sandra wasn't at all convinced but felt a little better for the reassurance. Her mother said goodbye to her on the landing outside the head's office.

'Remember now, it's the number 18 bus. Make sure you get off at the right stop and go straight home, and don't talk to any strange people.'

It wasn't the first time her mother had warned her about speaking to strangers. Sandra had been puzzled at first as she had always been brought up to greet all and sundry as a matter of courtesy, but she realised that in a big city, every stranger could potentially pose a deadly threat.

Then her mother set off down the stairs. For a moment Sandra felt desolate. She had a fleeting flashback in her mind's eye of herself at the age of eight standing on the pier at Kingston Harbour, waving to her mother as she sailed away.

'Don't leave me again, Mamma,' she wanted to shout, but no words came.

She made her way back to the head's office. Mr Francis stopped a girl who was passing the office. 'Caroline,' he said, 'this is Sandra, a new girl. Will you take her to class 2C?'

The dreaded moment had arrived. Sandra followed the girl down a flight of stairs and into a large hall. The girl ushered her into a classroom adjoining the hall where the teacher sat at a desk in front of a large blackboard. She had just finished taking the register.

The class fell silent as Sandra entered. The teacher, a thin bespectacled woman with red hair drawn up into a bun at the back of her head, motioned her to a desk that had been reserved for her at the back of the class. As she made her way to the desk, Sandra was painfully aware that she was the only black child in the class. She sat down amidst silence. She had never sat at the back of a class before. Granny had insisted that she sat at the front for she believed that it was only the dunces and time-wasters who sat at the back.

'We have a new member of our class,' the teacher said. 'Her name is Sandra James and she is from Jamaica.'

'Do they speak English in Jamaica, miss?' asked a boy.

'Perhaps Sandra can answer that question herself,' said the teacher.

'Pidgin English,' offered another boy before Sandra could say anything.

'I am sure Sandra can speak for herself,' said the teacher, obviously trying to help her put the record straight. But Sandra's heart pounded.

'Is English we speak in Jamaica,' said Sandra in her soft lilting accent.

There were sniggers in the class.

'Perhaps Sandra could tell us something about Jamaica later. The class would benefit, I am sure, by learning something about another country.'

'Do they live in trees, miss?' asked a boy amidst laughter.

'Do they wear grass skirts?' asked another.

'Do they live in mud huts?'

And so it went on.

Sandra held back the tears. She was old enough to know that any sign of weakness now would be exploited later by the children. She didn't trust her voice not to break if she spoke either, so she said nothing.

'That's quite enough,' chided Miss Claire. 'People have different customs in different parts of the world,' she added, trying to smooth things over. But Sandra felt Miss Claire's good intentions only served to confirm their belief that life in Jamaica was somehow strange.

Sandra wanted to say: no, we don't live in mud huts and we don't wear grass skirts and we can speak proper English. But she checked herself, for what if it *were* true? Would it make her any less worthy as a human being?

The class was doing an exercise in comprehension. Sandra could answer most of the questions but she daren't put her hand up. She was relieved when the bell for breaktime came. The children streamed noisily into the playground.

Only one girl remained behind. She approached Sandra. 'I'm Elaine.'

'Hello,' said Sandra, glad to see the friendly smile on her face.

'Aren't you coming out to the playground?'

'It's too cold outside,' said Sandra.

'You can't stay in here during breaktime,' she said. 'You'll soon get accustomed to the cold. And you ain't gonna make no friends by staying inside.'

Sandra understood Elaine's logic, but didn't much care to get accustomed to the cold or make friends.

'I'll come out later,' she said.

'All right then, I'll look out for you.'

Sandra spent a miserable fifteen minutes in the classroom on her own before classes started again.

When the bell went for lunch, Sandra was again determined to stay in the classroom. But this time Elaine was more insistent.

'Don't pay them no mind,' she said. 'They're just stupid.'

Sandra was starving so was easily persuaded. They joined the lunch queue with their metal trays and were helped to lashings of mashed potatoes, peas, soggy cabbage and 'toad in the hole', which was the largest sausage Sandra had ever seen, swimming in a sea of batter.

Sandra found the vegetables too bland for her taste but, to her surprise, liked the 'toad in the hole'.

After lunch most of the children wandered off into the playground. Sandra was grateful that Elaine stuck with her. Though Elaine was mild-mannered and didn't seem physically capable of protecting her from the bigger children, Sandra felt secure in her presence.

Elaine sat with her on a bench and asked her all sorts of questions but no silly questions about the customs in Jamaica. She took a packet of chewing gum from her pocket and offered a stick to Sandra. For a while they both sat on the bench without saying anything, their jaws moving up and down in unison. From time to time Elaine made a popping sound with the chewing gum.

'How do you do that?' queried Sandra.

For the rest of the break Sandra struggled with learning the technique of popping her chewing gum. For a while it seemed the most important thing in her life. When at last she managed to make the popping sound she was happy for the first time that day but then the bell rang to announce the afternoon school session. Sandra was glad when the end of the school day arrived and even more glad that Elaine could travel part of the way home with her.

As soon as the bus arrived there was a mad rush as the children headed for the upper deck. Sandra and Elaine got caught up in the scramble and were soon sitting side by side near the rear of the bus. Sandra hoped that she would have been able to sit at the very front and look out at the road below but those seats were already taken. Two boys sitting in front of them lit up a cigarette. Sandra noticed that the floor was littered with cigarette butts and that the air was stuffy with sweat and stale tobacco, but nothing could diminish the sense of adventure she felt.

All too soon Elaine's stop came.

'See you tomorrow, Sandra,' said Elaine as she hopped off the bus.

'See you,' said Sandra more cheerfully than she really felt

inside, for though she had made a friend, it didn't compensate for the hostility of some of the others.

On her own Sandra suddenly felt alone and vulnerable, but fortunately the other children ignored her. She recognised her stop and skipped off the bus and ran all the way home.

16 Alone

For the first time since arriving in England Sandra was alone. The house was like the inside of a fridge. She set about lighting the gas fire herself. Then she made herself a cup of tea and helped herself to a slice of bun. The English-style tea with milk added was still a novelty, but it warmed her insides as she sat huddled beside the fire watching television.

After a while she got bored with the television and turned it off, but immediately the memories of the day's events came flooding back. She sat glumly on the sofa for a while. Then she fetched her pen and the air letter form her dad had given her and sat down to write to Granny.

Sandra had never really enjoyed writing to her mother and father. They seemed so far away and their letters were almost always to Granny. Her mother usually wrote and her letters were cool and restrained, so Sandra's letters to them were somewhat stiff and impersonal.

She wrote her English address for the first time. She added the date, 18 November, 1966. She had never had to write to Granny before because she was always there. She conjured up a picture of her face.

Dearest Granny,

I arrived safely in England. I enjoyed the boat trip in the end but I didn't like the food at all. You wouldn't believe it but we had a real storm at sea. We saw some waves as tall as our tambrind tree. I thought we were going to sink but, thank goodness, the storm died down after a while. And guess what? The brown paper really worked so I was never seasick after that.

Mamma and Dadda and the twins met me at Southampton. The twins are sweet (most of the time, anyway) but they don't really understand that I am their sister and that they have a grandmother in Jamaica. They really look alike and speak alike, but in some ways they are not alike at all.

We went on the train to Waterloo Station. We took a taxi home and we passed Buckingham Palace but we didn't see the Queen. Today I went on a tall double-decker bus and sat upstairs all by myself. I was really scared though because I thought that the bus was going to topple over on its side when it went around a corner. You should see me holding on to the seat rail!

I really miss you, Granny. And Leroy too. Last night I had a dream about you. I dreamt that I was high up on a cliff and that you were standing beside me and you said you were going to teach me to fly. And at the end of the dream I was flying like a bird.

Oh, Granny, I wish you could send for me. I hate England. But most of all I hate school. The children tease me and call me names. I wish that I never left Jamaica and I want to come back home.

I don't want you to worry about me so please don't be sad, but it's just that I don't have anybody to tell my feelings to so I hope you will understand that I am just writing my thoughts down on paper to get things off my chest or I will explode (smile).

England is very cold. Dadda says there is a cold spell on now but it won't always be so cold. I think he is only saying that so to make me feel better. He says it might snow when it gets nearer to Christmas time. I don't think I would mind the snow too much though because at least it will be pretty.

I must stop now because I am running out of space. I hope that you are missing me because I am missing you very, very much. Please please, Granny, write to me soon.

> Lots and
> lots and
> lots of love and kisses,
> Sandra

PS Thank you for packing Lizzie.

She licked the gummed flaps and sealed it before addressing it. She hated air letter forms and remembered how hard they were to open for Granny. Sandra decided there and then that she was going to buy a writing pad and some airmail envelopes so that she could write proper letters to Granny.

She put on her coat and slipped out the front door to the post-box at the end of the street. She had hardly got back home when her father returned from work.

'You found your way back OK?'

'Yes, Elaine came with me part of the way.'

'Who is Elaine?'

'She's a friend I made.'

'A black girl?'

'No, she white.'

'And what about school? Everything went OK?'

Before Sandra could answer the twins charged into the flat.

'These children will be the death of me,' Mother panted, leaning the folded push-chair against the passage wall.

'You get along fine at school?' she asked. 'You managed to find your way back home OK?' she continued, rolling two questions into one.

'Yes, Mum,' said Sandra answering the second question only.

The twins made further conversation impossible. Wayne was chasing Jean with a jet aeroplane propelled in two outstretched hands and roaring like a Mig fighter, and Jean was dashing in and out around them.

'Children, be quiet!' shrieked their mother but they either didn't hear or just chose to ignore her and in the end she gave up and disappeared into the kitchen to start to prepare the evening meal. Sandra was relieved for she didn't want to have to talk about her day at school.

She headed for the bedroom but found the doorway barred by Wayne. With both hands extended to the full and with both feet splayed out, he just managed to span the door frame. Jean was hiding behind the door but her barely suppressed giggling made it clear to Sandra that she was definitely an accomplice.

'You can't come in,' said Wayne.

'You can't,' said Jean from behind the door, laughing as if it were the biggest joke in the world.

Sandra folded her arms and tried her best to look sullen yet defiant, as if she was prepared to wait there till they let her through. But she hadn't figured on Jean taking up her post beside Wayne as assistant gatekeeper.

'It's our room,' said Jean, sticking out her tongue defiantly.

'Don't stick out your tongue,' said Sandra, remembering one of Granny's strictures. 'It's not nice.'

Jean and Wayne stood looking at each other as if they were hatching some wicked plot. They slowly, as if on a dare, started to stick out their tongues.

Sandra had had enough of their game and decided to brush past them and enter the room. But Wayne and Jean weren't giving up so easily and in the end Sandra had to forcibly extricate her knees to move.

Wayne and Jean were hysterical with laughter as she finally shook them off in triumph. But no sooner had she got to her bed than Jean began to cry.

'She hurted me, she hurted me,' extending her right hand, 'Mummy, Mummy, Sandra hurted my hand. It's bleeding.'

'Don't be silly,' said Sandra.

'Look, there's blood!'

'I can't see any blood.'

'Look,' said Jean, extending her hand for Sandra to inspect.

'Where's the blood?' said Sandra impatiently.

'There . . .'

'Where?'

'Can't you see, silly. There!'

Sandra took Jean's hand and peered at the spot and just laughed.

'It's not funny,' said Wayne.

'You're laughing,' said Jean and started to wail all the more.

Before Sandra knew it her mother was at the door. 'Sandra, what's going on in here? Jean, I hear you say you cut yourself?'

'It's just her imagination,' Sandra got in quickly.

'Let me have a look at that hand.'

'I need a plaster,' wailed Jean.

'It's OK. You don't need a plaster.'

'Yes, Mum, I do.'

'OK then, Sandra will put a plaster on for you. Sandra, take her to the bathroom and put a plaster on, please.'

'I don't want Sandra to put it on. I want you to put it on, Mum.'

'Oh, God give me strength,' said her mother. 'All right, all right, I will put it on.'

'I want one too,' said Wayne.

'OK, OK, you too. Come with me, both of you.'

'You haven't told Sandra off, Mum.'

'Sandra is sharing your room now. You must both learn to share.'

'You haven't told off Sandra, Mum,' chipped in Wayne.

'You listen to me, Wayne, the same goes for you as for Jean. You must both learn to share with Sandra. After all Sandra shares her doll with you.'

'She doesn't,' said Wayne, pointing to Lizzie. Lizzie was resting at the bottom of Sandra's bed.

Her mother looked at Sandra with reproachful eyes.

'You must tell her off,' wailed Jean whose stamping carried with it the seeds of a tantrum.

'No, I will not,' said Mum crossly and swiftly turned to Sandra and said in a voice that was precariously poised between a command and a plea, 'Please, Sandra. Just take it easy with them. Remember that they are only little.'

The twins immediately lost interest in the proceedings and headed for Lizzie. Their mother slipped away before they could remember that they needed plasters.

Sandra knew that her mother had realised it was only a trivial incident but she felt slighted and upset that even the smallest thing could trigger off irrational feelings of rejection and isolation.

Later at dinner, after the twins had been put to bed, the subject of school resurfaced, but this time her parents were more probing.

'Don't pay them any mind,' said her mum after Sandra told them of the day's events.

'And just get on with your schoolwork,' added her father.

When she got to school the next day she immediately sought out Elaine. But Elaine wasn't there. Panic set in.

At first Sandra thought Elaine was just late, but later it was clear that she was not coming to school. You can never depend on people, she thought. They always desert you when you need them most. But perhaps she was being hasty, there was probably some good reason for her absence. Worrying about Elaine on top of everything else didn't do much for her confidence as the bell announced the first break.

She decided to go to the toilet and idled most of the breaktime away. Afterwards she made her way back to the classroom where she spent the rest of the break on her own. After lunch she headed straight for the classroom. But this time she was intercepted by a teacher she hadn't met before, who told her that children were not allowed in the classroom during breaktimes but must go out to the playground. So she edged her way into the playground, trying to make herself invisible. Her obvious lack of confidence, as much as her colour, only helped to make her conspicuous and before long there was a sea of jeering faces around her.

'Look who's here!'

'It's the golliwog.'

'Hello, golliwog.'

'Hello, blackie.'

'Where do you come from, blackie?'

'Why don't you go back to where you come from?'

'To your mud hut!'

Sandra looked in the direction of the teacher on break duty.

As the group gathered round her, a boy quietly crept up behind her and crouched down and another boy shoved her so that she fell backwards over the crouched figure. She landed on her behind but managed to break her fall with outstretched hands.

She quickly regained her feet amidst laughter.

She stood defiantly, facing the crowd as if daring them to repeat the prank. But inside she didn't feel anywhere near as brave.

'I'll tell teacher,' she said.

'I'll tell teacher!' they mimicked in unison.

'Go on then,' said a girl, giving her a hefty shove. 'Go on and tell.'

Sandra wished she hadn't issued a threat. If she told the teacher her life would be hell, but if she didn't tell the teacher she would have no credibility and her life would be hell just the same. She decided that she had to go through with her threat.

She stormed off in the direction of the teacher, whose name she didn't know.

'They're shoving me and calling me names, sir!' she said.

'Who are "they"?' enquired the teacher.

'Them, sir,' said Sandra, turning in the direction she came from. But the crowd that had gathered round her had dispersed and the children were once again spread out over the playground.

'If you ignore them,' the teacher said, 'they will just get tired of calling you names.'

Ignore them! As far as Sandra was concerned it was already too late for they had all seen her go over to the teacher. If the teacher didn't take any action, they would have gained a kind of victory. And he didn't. Sandra made her way dejectedly to the classroom.

She gathered her school things together and hung out in the hallway until she heard the bell ending the lunch break. In the confusion of children returning to the classrooms, Sandra slipped out into the playground and darted unseen through the gates of the school.

Half an hour later she was warming her hands in her front room and watching television, hoping to lose herself behind a veil of forgetfulness.

When over dinner her mum and dad asked her about school she simply said, 'Everything is fine. Just fine.'

17 'My thoughts are with you'

'Where were you yesterday?' Sandra asked accusingly.

'Kevin was sick, that's my little brother, and me mum couldn't get time off work to look after him, so I had to stay at home.'

'Oh,' said Sandra, relieved that there was good cause for Elaine to be away. 'Is he better now?'

'Oh yes, he had a tummy upset, that's all.'

'Oh, I see.'

'Anything happened yesterday?' enquired Elaine, sensing that something was amiss. Sandra told her.

'Who was it?' inquired Elaine aggressively, but Sandra didn't know the names of her tormentors. Just as well, thought Sandra, as she didn't want the situation to be inflamed. She was glad however for Elaine's support.

They had a double art lesson and she stuck as close as she could to Elaine.

'She's nice,' said Elaine.

'Who?' inquired Sandra as the whole class noisily made their way up the crowded staircase to the art room occasionally sidestepping marauding fourth- and sixth-year students on their way downstairs.

'Miss Rigby, the art teacher.'

'Is she?' said Sandra, probing.

'Yeah. She's really with it.'

'With what?'

'With it.'

'It what?'

'With it!' she laughed, suddenly remembering that Sandra had just come up from Jamaica. 'You know, dead trendy!'

'Oh, I see,' said Sandra, 'you mean that she is in style.'

Miss Rigby was 'trendy' all right, compared to the other 'square' teachers who dressed conservatively. She wore a pair of sunshine yellow trousers with a white floral pattern and a yellow top. A pair of bright red costume-jewellery earrings dangled from her ears and her hair was a mass of curls which cascaded down to her shoulders.

The art room was on the third floor overlooking the playground. The sun streamed through the large windows and gave the room a light airy atmosphere. Sandra felt a surge of excitement. In Jamaica she had never had the chance to do much more than crayon drawings in her exercise book because only private schools had the sort of equipment she now saw in the art room.

'You are new,' Sandra heard Miss Rigby saying to her in a friendly, welcoming sort of way.

'Yes, miss,' said Sandra guardedly.

'She's just come up from Jamaica,' Elaine intervened.

'Right then, I'll have to set you some work.' She told the class to continue with the project they were working on and after they were settled she came round to Sandra again.

'Do you like painting then?' she queried.

'I haven't done much before,' replied Sandra, speaking as correctly as she could.

'Have you ever tried working with powder paints?' Miss Rigby probed.

'No,' replied Sandra. She had only ever used some water-colours from a paint set Leroy was sent from England one Christmas.

Miss Rigby took a spoonful of red powder from a can and showed Sandra the right amount of water to mix in with it to get a good consistency. Under her supervision, Sandra prepared a variety of colours starting with the primary colours of red, blue and yellow.

'Now that the colours are ready you have to choose a subject matter. The rest of the class are working on portraits of their family. Is there anybody in your family you want to paint?'

Sandra looked round and saw that some of the class were working from photographs they had brought with them. 'I didn't bring a picture of anybody.'

'Well, have a go just the same. You'll have to use your imagination.'

Sandra was silent for a while trying to figure out who to draw.

'What about your mum?' prompted Miss Rigby. 'Or perhaps your dad,' she added tentatively, as if uncertain as to whether Sandra was from a one-parent family or not.

For some reason Sandra didn't want to draw her mum or dad.

'I'll paint my granny,' she said with sudden decisiveness.

'Is she here in England?'

'She's in Jamaica.'

'That sounds like a good idea. You can have a practice run now and perhaps you could bring in a photograph next week and start again.'

Sandra tried to conjure up in her mind the photograph that was in her parents' bedroom of Granny sitting in the photographer's studio with a large potted fern in the background.

'Start off by drawing the picture, and when you are satisfied then you can apply the paint.' Miss Rigby then wandered off to attend to the other students.

Sandra didn't manage to capture any convincing resemblance to Granny on the paper, but she was nonetheless comforted by the vision of Granny that she held in her head while she struggled with the drawing.

From time to time Miss Rigby peered over her shoulder while she struggled with the drawing, and Sandra spent almost as much time using the eraser as the pencil. Occasionally Miss Rigby interrupted and gave her advice on the anatomy of the human head.

When Sandra had finished the drawing to her satisfaction she set about applying colour to it.

'Don't apply the colour too thickly,' advised Miss Rigby, 'just build the colours up in thin layers. That way you have more control and the skin tone will look more convincing.'

Sandra struggled with the new technique and, following Miss

Rigby's advice, she carefully built up the colour on Granny's face, allowing time for each layer to dry before proceeding to the next.

By the time Miss Rigby came around again she was well into the painting.

'By the way,' Miss Rigby said nonchalantly, 'what colour is your granny?'

Sandra was mystified. She had never before consciously attempted to define Granny's colour by putting it into words. In Jamaica people were usually described as being dark- or light-skinned or even red-skinned. But these categories were necessarily vague because of the wide range of skin tones around and because much depended on the person using them. In England she had only heard talk of 'black' and 'white'.

'She's sort of brown,' said Sandra, neatly sidestepping any precise definition.

'Well then, look at the colours there in front of you.' Miss Rigby pointed at the jars of powdered paint stocked on a table. 'Look at this burnt umber, and this gorgeous sienna brown. And here is a lovely vandyke brown! Mix them with yellow ochre, or with vermilion red or any other colour that suits your fancy and you'd be surprised how many shades of brown you can get.'

Sandra realised that, without thinking, she had painted Granny in a powdery shade of pink. Maybe she was ashamed of Granny's colour. If so, was she ashamed of her own colour, too, which was even darker than Granny's? It wasn't that she minded being black, she just didn't want to be different from the other children at school, and painting Granny paler than she was must have been a way of expressing this wish. She felt ashamed that, in a roundabout sort of way, she had disowned Granny. She was angry with herself, angry with school and angry with England.

She stayed on after the end of the class and repainted the portrait, putting on layers of the various shades of brown Miss Rigby had suggested. Sandra had to admit to herself that the paintings didn't look much like Granny, but for some reason she felt excited. She wasn't quite able to put her feelings into words but she knew that, in some sort of fumbling way, she had crossed another river.

'Not a bad first attempt at a portrait,' Miss Rigby said, studying the painting. 'Next week you can bring the photograph and work directly from it. That should make things much easier.'

Sandra left the class with a light head. She skipped down the steps and headed to the playground in search of Elaine. Sandra spotted her at the corner of the playground with two of her friends. She hesitated, not wishing to intrude, but Elaine saw her and called her over. The other girls briefly acknowledged her, but soon drifted away. Sandra speculated that perhaps they didn't like her, or might have been afraid of being victimised by the others if seen with her. Or perhaps it was their turn to feel like intruders.

Alone with Elaine, Sandra braced herself for trouble.

'Let's play hopscotch,' suggested Elaine, moving towards the painted squares on the playground. Sandra's first instinct was to say no. Not only had she outgrown hopscotch, she thought, but the squares were in the middle of the playground and it would have been like moving to the front line of a battlefield. She had second thoughts however and followed Elaine and enjoyed herself.

As they made their way back to the classroom, she decided the best way of heading off trouble was to act as if you didn't expect it to come your way. In fact the taunting lessened. Sandra was relieved, though in her bones she felt it was nothing but the lull before the storm.

Granny's letter arrived about two weeks later as she was leaving for school. She read it on the bus.

My dear Sandra,
   Yours I received Wednesday last and I hope that you and all the family keeping well. I glad to hear you reach England safe and sound and up till now I still giving thanks that the Good Lord deliver you from a storm on your sea passage always remembering He is our Father and if we leave everything in His hands then take courage in His words, 'I will never leave or forsake you when all else fail'. You see

*I was right that the brown paper good for seasickness so there
you are your old Granny knows a thing or two. I am truly
sorry to hear that you not getting along so wonderful at
school but we all have our trials in this life trust in the Lord
and pray that things will get better. Whatever name people
call you, you must not forget who you are and where you come
from. Your father had to work hard to get to England to
better himself and he and your mother sacrifice to send for you
so that you can go to a good school and get a good education
and have a better chance in life so you must buckle down and
take advantage of the opportunity life present to you.
Remember that England is now your home and you must try
your best to settle down. Your mother and father are with
you now so you must make sure that they know how things
are going with you in school. Leroy is fine and sends his love.
Only yesterday the price of flour and cooking oil gone up and
with prices everywhere sky high only God knows how we will
manage. What can you do but hope and pray. Next time you
write I hope things will be better with you. I am far but my
thoughts are with you from the break of day till the setting of
the sun at night. Give my love to Mamma and Dadda and
kiss Wayne and Jean for me. Tell them that their Granmother
send to say howdy.*

    God Bless you.
    Granny.

Sandra read the letter again. Granny had such faith in God
and in England as a land of boundless opportunity! But would
Granny think the same if she was living in England? Would she
think that the schools were so wonderful if she had to go to one
every day? And how can you learn if children keep calling you
names?

In her mind Sandra began to compose the letter which she
would write to Granny until Elaine interrupted her.

'I see you got a letter,' said Elaine, eyeing the letter Sandra held
in her hand.

'It's from my granny.'

'From Jamaica?'

'Yes.'

'I bet you miss her?'

Sandra nodded. 'I used to live with her before I came up.'

'My gran used to live down the road from us then they knocked down all the houses. She an' Grandad are now living on an estate about ten miles away. They hate it.'

Elaine made it sound very far away. Sandra wished that Granny was only ten miles away.

'Is she all right then?' probed Elaine.

'Oh yes, she's fine and so is Leroy.'

'He'll soon be over, I suppose.'

'I hope so.'

They were silent for a while. Sandra wished that it was a different kind of letter and that she could have shared more of its contents with Elaine. She wondered too about Granny's writing with hardly a full stop or a comma or a new paragraph and couldn't figure out if Granny was trying to cram as much writing as she could into the air letter or if it was because she didn't know better.

In her mind she saw their house and tried to imagine the sleeping figures of Granny and Leroy curled up in their beds. Elaine had to nudge her out of her daydreaming for they had reached their stop. Sandra had made an uneasy peace with her classmates: they ignored her and she ignored them.

It didn't take her long to realise that she was in the low stream for the second year. Class A did more advanced work and a much higher standard of work was expected from them. At first she had accepted it with resignation for it was not her habit to question the decision of her teachers or grown-ups. She simply assumed that there was such a high standard of education in England that she would have to work very hard to catch up. But soon she came to realise that she was more advanced in some subjects than the other children in her class. Some of them could hardly read or write. She couldn't believe it at first as in Jamaica you wouldn't get to the second year unless you had achieved the minimum level set for the first year and to be kept down was to be labelled a dunce. She realised that in England you were moved up by age and not performance, but if your work wasn't up to scratch you were placed in a lower stream for that year group.

But why was she in the lower stream? Nobody had tested her. It was either assumed that she would not be able to cope with the work in the A stream or nobody cared if she was held back. Not much was expected of the children in her class and by and large they lived up to that expectation. They formed little groups and chatted away during class or read comics or even played card games and the teachers let them as long as they were not disruptive. Sandra didn't find the work challenging and after a while boredom set in. Soon boredom gave way to slow nagging anger that smouldered with a slow fuse.

One day after lunch she found herself alone in a corner of the playground, waiting for Elaine to join her, and trying her best not to attract attention to herself. Some children were playing football and by chance the ball was kicked in her direction. It came to rest against the railings behind her and Karen, a big-boned white girl, bounded over to retrieve it and noticed that Sandra was on her own.

Instead of picking up the ball she gave it a hefty kick against the railings and it ricocheted and hit Sandra's legs. This was the cue for another boy, Jason, to repeat the action and this time the ball narrowly missed her.

Just then Elaine came on the scene and rushed over to Sandra's defence.

'Stop that, you!' she shrieked.

'Mind your own business!' retorted Jason.

'It is my business!'

'In that case, take this!' He kicked the ball straight at Elaine and as she took evasive action the ball struck her on her back.

The ball flew off the railings and came to a rest by Sandra. She took it up and made to hurl it at Jason. Then she froze. She stood there for what seemed an eternity with the ball held aloft. Their eyes met and held each other in a stare.

The playground fell silent as all eyes were focused on Sandra.

Waiting expectant eyes that willed Sandra to hurl the ball at Jason and start the fight which was bound to follow as night follows day.

It was Elaine who diffused the tension.

'Don't waste time on them, Sandra,' she said, walking away and beckoning Sandra to follow.

Sandra held his stare for a few more seconds before releasing the ball. As she walked away she heard the ball bouncing on the concrete, the bounces increasing in rapidity till the ball trickled down the slope to a standstill.

'Stupid monkey!' he shouted. Then as a parting shot, 'We'll be waiting for you after school.'

Sandra sat through the afternoon classes with rising anxiety, hardly daring to take her eyes off the clock on the classroom wall.

Ten minutes before class ended she asked to be excused to go to the toilet. The teacher was reluctant to let her go so near to the end of the class, but misread the look of anxiety on Sandra's face as a sign of urgency, and let her go.

Sandra slipped out, discreetly clutching her school bag. She never returned. By the time the bell went to end the class and school for the day, she was already on the bus and halfway home.

When she got home she went straight to the bedroom and threw herself on the bed, face down. Her arm came to rest against Lizzie resting against the bedstead. She seized Lizzie by the arm and tossed her across the room. Lizzie crashed against the wall with a loud thud, then fell to the floor in a sad heap. Her left arm was dislodged and ended up on the other side of the room near the bottom bunk.

The next day she went in early to avoid any reception committee at the gate. During playtime however, she began to think that her fears were unfounded because Karen, Jason and the gang kept their distance. Perhaps it was because she stuck close to Elaine. Perhaps her tormentors were beginning to think that she was no push-over and that perhaps she might just fight back. Or maybe it was still just the lull before the storm?

There was no time to find out that term, for before they knew it, the Christmas holiday was upon them.

18 Christmas

Dear Granny,

Thank you for your letter. I am sorry that I am not replying till now but I was very busy with my schoolwork and also with helping out with the twins. Every day after school I pick them up from the child-minder, as that saves some money which can go towards buying the house. Sometimes when Mamma is late from work I fix their supper and put them to bed. Now that it is holiday time the twins don't go to the child-minder and I look after them during the day, so I don't have much time for writing letters.

Things are a little better at school but I still have some trouble with the children calling me names. Some of the subjects are new to me and it is very difficult to catch up but I am trying my best.

Guess what, Granny? I did a picture of you and it is now hanging over my bed.

I hope that you and Leroy are fine. Dadda works a lot in the nights because he is always doing overtime so I don't see him much except at weekends. He says that after we buy a house Leroy will come up.

I am getting more accustomed to the cold and I hope that it will snow at Christmas so that I can see what it looks like. Wayne and Jean are sweet but they can be little devils when they want to be. I am sure I will get on better with them when I have my own room.

I am not getting on so well in my school as I find the lessons boring and some of the subjects are new to me. A few of the

*teachers think I am stupid because I don't like to speak in class
and I don't ask questions. Mamma says that I am not making a
big enough effort to fit in but it is not like Jamaica where the
teachers make sure you work hard. I tell Mamma this but
she says that since I come to England I turn lazy, but I know
that is not true. I really wish I was back in my old school and
that I had my old teachers back.*

*England is not as bad as at first but I still wish I was back in
Jamaica with you. Give my love to Leroy and tell him I will
write him soon. I hope you have a lovely Christmas. I will miss
you.*

> *Lots and lots of love and kisses,*
> *Sandra*

Sandra folded the letter, placed it in the envelope then addressed
it. She congratulated herself on her timing, for no sooner had she
finished than her father returned home from his night shift which
allowed Sandra and her mother to set off on their weekly
Saturday shopping trip, leaving the twins in his care. They were
going to buy the twins their Christmas present.

Her mother had already started to do some of her Christmas
shopping though Christmas was three weeks away.

Sandra couldn't imagine Christmas without Granny and
certainly not without her rich, fruity Christmas cake. In January
of each year, Granny would get out a large glass container and fill
it with currants, raisins, sultanas and cherries, over which she
would pour a quantity of rum. The container would then be
sealed and left to soak till Christmas, when the fruit provided the
main ingredients of her Christmas cake.

Curiously Sandra didn't feel the Christmas spirit in spite of
the frosted shop windows, decorated with holly and ivy, and the
Christmas trees lit up with fairy lights that appeared in the
windows of houses. Perhaps it was because there were no roving
masquerade bands making music with fife and drums and no
'horse head' scaring children with their pranks; no jingles on the
radio reminding listeners that there were only fourteen shopping
days left before Christmas, and the pitch of excitement when

there was only one day to go before Christmas. Nor were there a medley of Christmas carols on the radio throughout the day; no noisy firecrackers set off by schoolchildren.

By the time they got back home, her father had already given the twins their lunch. He pounced: 'What tek' you all so long? You know how long I waiting to go to sleep now?'

'Is not ordinary shopping I have to do, you know. Is Christmas shopping!' retorted her mother.

'Christmas season barely start and look how much money you spend already! Anybody would think money going out of style and you figuring out how to get rid of it as quick as you can!'

'There are the children to think about even if you give up on Christmas.'

'You seem, more excited 'bout it than them.'

'Listen to who talking! When we sit down to eat Christmas dinner is you same one going to be stuffing yourself more than anybody else!'

'I don't have anything against a good Christmas dinner but you know how money tight. We don't have to have everything! We don't have to have turkey and chicken and ham and acree an' saltfish and every blessed thing!'

'Dennis, your daughter come up from Jamaica and you don't want us to have a decent Christmas dinner!'

That shamed him into silence for a moment. Then he added in a conciliatory tone, 'Don't forget there is Leroy to come too! On top of that we have to scrape up enough money for a deposit on a house . . .'

'I know all that,' interrupted her mother, 'but a few little extras for Christmas not going to break the bank.'

'All right, all right,' he said, 'but we can't have everything, you know. So everybody better tighten their belt an' start to turn off the lights when they not in the room and we don't need the gas heater going all hours when the house not cold. Otherwise we'll never get out of this dump!' He stormed out of the room and went to bed.

All that Sandra could think was that England had changed her father. Somehow she felt better if she could blame England. This cold wretched country that took the light out of people's eyes! Her father wasn't the same happy-go-lucky father she remembered. Now he had no close friends, never went to the pub for a drink and didn't even seem to approve when her mother's friends visited. His only concerns seemed to be with money, with working long hours of overtime and with turning off lights and penny-pinching.

She tried her best to understand his need to save to get enough for a deposit on a house. When she felt cold at home or when he had bawled her out for not turning off the light, she reminded herself that it was all in a good cause. A house meant Leroy coming up, it meant getting her own room, it meant the future happiness of the entire family.

Even though her father was often away at nights and asleep during much of the time he was at home, he somehow dominated the household. the television and record player had to be turned down low and the twins had to play quietly. Their mother was always shushing them: 'Quiet! Don't wake up your father,' or warning Sandra: 'Turn off the heater before your father come home and catch you wasting gas.'

Sometimes on a Saturday morning when they were all at home and he hadn't yet come home from his night shift, there would be a light and happy atmosphere in the house with the twins playing noisily and their mother pottering about. Yet the minute they heard their father's key in the door the atmosphere would change.

Sandra believed that there was something out there in the city, where he went to work at night, which was intent on devouring his heart and soul. There was some indignity or humiliation, which turned to anger and resentment the minute he put his key into the front-door lock, and which hardened into mean thoughts and harsh words to bruise his family.

But not all the changes in him were for the worse. It had taken Sandra a little while to get accustomed to the sight of him cooking, or washing dishes, or vacuuming the carpet, or pushing the twins in the push-chair. These tasks were considered women's work in Jamaica. In fact Sandra couldn't wait till Leroy got to

England when he would have to do his fair share of housework. Good!

A few days later, the postman delivered a round parcel addressed to her. The minute she felt its weight, and saw the Jamaican postmark, she knew it was one of Granny's Christmas cakes. She felt a warm glow inside. Christmas wasn't going to be so bad after all.

And it wasn't.

As Christmas approached there was a thaw in the weather and she wasn't sure if it was her imagination, but she felt she was at last getting the Christmas spirit. If only it snowed, thought Sandra, then London would begin to be like the familiar Christmas cards. On Christmas Eve she and her mother even came across a choir outside an underground station, holding lighted candles and singing all her favourite carols.

'We're going to church tomorrow morning,' her mother announced after they had had dinner and the twins had been put to bed.

'Count me out,' said her father.

'It's Christmas, Dennis.'

'I can't be bothered with no church.'

'It's years now since we ain't been to church. Not since the twins had their christening.'

'You know the hours I work?'

'I know it's difficult, but you not working tomorrow.'

'How come you so interested in church all of a sudden?'

'I keep telling you, it's Christmas. It would be nice, now that Sandra is here, if we all went to church.'

'You forget what it was like first time we went.'

'Things are changing . . .'

'I can remember when the parson say, "Let us offer one another a sign of peace." Suddenly all the white people gone blind!'

'Well, it may be different now.'

'You may be right, but I don't think I want to give anybody

110

he chance to snub me. Sandra, don't mind me. Is just that this country too ungodly.'

'An' you making it worse. Well, me and Sandra going to church with the twins first thing in the morning, aren't we, Sandra?'

'Yes, Mum.'

'An' we going to say a little prayer for your father's soul.'

'Well, I might just decide to get the Christmas spirit.' He got up and went to the drinks cabinet and took out a bottle of rum and fetched a can of Coke from the fridge.

'Oh, I see. Is that sort of spirit you mean.'

'Appleton,' he said, looking fondly at the bottle, 'the best rum in the world.' He poured two rum and Cokes and a Coke for Sandra. 'Come on,' he coaxed, 'join the sinner in a Christmas drink.'

Sandra followed Mum's lead and took the drink.

'Merry Christmas,' he toasted, raising the glass.

'Merry Christmas.'

'Merry Christmas.'

'You must be missing your grandmother and Leroy, eh, Sandra?' he said, easing her into the conversation.

'Yes,' said Sandra. 'Is the first Christmas I going to spend without seeing them.'

'Is six years now I don't see my mother and son.' Sandra had forgotten that he too nursed his own private grief.

'Christmas is for children,' he said cheerfully as if he had just made an important discovery. 'And, Sandra, I going to see to it that you children have a merry Christmas.'

'That's nice, Dadda.' Sandra could see that he was trying to lift their spirits and was trying her best to support his efforts.

'When I was a boy,' he said, 'we didn't have much, but I can tell you we used to really enjoy weself at Christmas.' That started him off on a nostalgic journey down memory lane which lasted well into the night.

As midnight approached he said, 'We better go to bed now, we have to be up in the morning.'

Sandra didn't forget to wear her hat to church. She had avoided the subject of church in her letters to Granny so as not to upset her. Now she could write and say that they had all been to church on Christmas morning and that they sang her favourite carols. Even her father, she thought, enjoyed the service though he feigned indifference.

After church it was time to open their presents. The sight of the presents under a real fir Christmas tree was still a novelty to her. Back home they had always made do with a tree made from crêpe paper folded over a wire frame.

She was very pleased with her present from her mum and dad, which was a watch with a slim leather band. In addition she got some clothes, including a mini skirt. The twins got an assortment of toys and clothes, but were much keener on the toys.

Christmas dinner was traditional Jamaican and exactly as Granny would have prepared it, with the exception of the turkey. Granny maintained that a turkey was much too big for just herself, Leroy and Sandra, though Sandra guessed that she wasn't particularly fond of turkey anyway. Now that Sandra had tasted turkey for the first time she wasn't impressed, and suspected that without liberal dollops of cranberry sauce it would be pretty tasteless.

The turkey reminded her of the times when, on their way to the sea, she and Leroy used to pass a yard where turkeys were kept behind high wire-mesh cages. They teased them by mimicking their gobbling sound, and the idiotic birds, like a bunch of parrots, never failed to take the bait and, fluffing out their feathers, would answer in chorus: gobble gobble gobble gobble gobble gobble . . .

Dinner ended with Granny's Christmas cake, which was served with lashings and lashings of brandy sauce. Her father was in a relaxed mood and couldn't stop praising Granny's baking.

After dinner he dusted off his collection of records and played a nostalgic medley of old Duke Ellington and Count Basie jazz standards, interspersed with ballads by Nat King Cole, Ella Fitzgerald, Ray Charles and other 'golden oldies' as her father called them. She hadn't seen this side of her father at all and didn't even know that he liked music.

The music, the mellow glow from the gas fire, the sparkling lights from the Christmas tree, the scent of pine blended with the aroma of her father's slender panatella cigars he was smoking for the occasion, the happy, smiling faces around her, all conspired to convince Sandra that Christmas in England was not so bad after all.

On the day after Boxing Day, they went to a party thrown by one of her mother's friends at the hospital where she worked. She was a nurse who lived in a terrace house with her husband and two daughters.

Sandra hadn't been to a proper grown-up party before with food and music and dancing. They had planned to travel there by underground and come back by taxi, and were walking to the station when her father, in a moment of recklessness, hailed a cab. 'Christmas comes but once a year,' he said with a flourish, waving them into the taxi. For a moment, Sandra thought he might have been a bit tipsy.

Though it was a party in a private house, they had to pay at the door. Sandra learned later that this was a practice amongst West Indians going back to the early days when few could afford to throw a party without sharing the cost.

They left their coats in an upstairs bedroom, deposited the twins in another room for the younger ones and went down to the dimly lit front room. Music blared from two gigantic speakers. There was a mass of swaying bodies moving in time to the music. The sofa and chairs were occupied by stout imperious women looking on with apparent boredom, but Sandra guessed that they were taking in everything.

Her father bought drinks for them, wine for her mother, orange squash for Sandra, and a drink for himself called 'mannish man' which Sandra hadn't heard of before.

As time passed more people came. Sandra was glad that there were a lot of other girls her age at the party. Unlike the older women, the girls didn't wait to be asked to dance and formed a little group, dancing by themselves. One of the older girls motioned her to join the group. She was shy, but her mother gave her an encouraging shove.

And that was how she came to spend half the night bopping

113

away to the rhythms of calypso and reggae and soul music. The DJ skilfully interspersed the calypso, favoured by the older folk, with the reggae and soul music that the young ones screamed for, and everybody was satisfied. Young and old alike fanned themselves, and wiped perspiration from their glistening faces, flushed with the happiness and drifting far, far away from the crushing weight and inhibitions of white society. They clapped and praised the DJ at the end of a good number and screamed, 'One more time.' One particular tune found favour with young and old alike and they all joined in the chorus:

> By the rivers of Babylon, where we sat down,
> There we wept, when we remembered Zion,
> For the wicked carried us away captivity,
> Required from us a song.
> How can we be thinking of a song in a strange land?

As the night wore on, soul music took over: Diana Ross and the Supremes, Sam an' Dave, Aretha Franklyn, Otis Redding, Wilson Pickett. Just when the party reached fever pitch, and perspiration was flowing freely down Sandra's face, there was a break for food. Curried goat and rice was served on paper plates.

Her mother and father were in good party spirit and chatted with her and with their friends. Had it not been for the twins they would probably have stayed for longer. As they were leaving, the party was entering a more sedate, intimate phase. The room was now darker, the music slow and romantic. Couples clung to each other and swayed rhythmically to the beat. As Sandra helped find the coats and get the twins ready, her parents disappeared once more into the room for a last dance. When she went to fetch them, they were dancing together like a pair of love birds. Sandra was both delighted and embarrassed at the same time.

They took a taxi home. Wayne and Jean were fast asleep and her mother and father struggled to carry them upstairs. Finally, Sandra crashed down on her bed, her head roaring with the sounds of her first Christmas party in England.

A few days into the new year Granny's letter arrived.

Dearest Sandra,

Another year I am thankful to God that my health is again with me after a little sickness I had. I feel lonely at heart that I don't have you to talk with but I must be contented I can get your letters and Leroy is still here with me and your Uncle Bertie still comes regularly. He is always anxious over me and Leroy. We just have to pray that everything work for the good. We had a nice Christmas we were invited to spend Boxing Day at Mrs Simpson then come New Year and Leroy spend a few days with your Uncle Bertie and his new girlfriend name Madge. They are to marry in the new year and I am looking forward to the wedding and will keep a reception for him here at home. I hope the Christmas cake reach you safe. Thank your Mamma and Dadda for the presents they send for me and Leroy and when I think of their kindness and love for us my eyes are filled with tears for all the good things God has done for me. Sandra I don't want to hear you say that you bored in school for if your teacher them not interested in you then your school books must be your teacher and if things seem too hard for you you must just raise your thoughts above and ask for help. That is prayer. He always hears us in our darkest hour and our faith grows stronger and our burden lighter. You must not be too tired with your old Granny but it give me a certain sweetness to write like this to you as if we are talking face to face so bear with me. It would do Mamma and Dadda heart proud if they could see how Leroy growing up tall even since you leave. He is working very hard in school and God willing will take his School Certificate exam next year as he will move up into class four when school start next week. Mas' Ken just take sick and die last week and we still shocked for he was hale and hearty one minute and the next minute he dead but the Lord giveth and the Lord taketh away.

Lots of love to you and yours and write soon.
Your Grandmother

19 The Test

Sandra's first morning of the Easter term brought her crashing down to earth. She felt a churning sensation in her stomach as she entered the school gates.

At playtime Sandra and Elaine, glad to see each other after the Christmas break, exchanged accounts of what they had done over the holiday. Sandra was sorry that she hadn't seen Elaine over the holidays but neither of them had a phone at home which made communication difficult. Sandra thought it funny that Elaine had never invited her to her home. Elaine was so free of any prejudice that Sandra found it difficult to imagine her parents as being any different.

She had to wait till Thursday for art class and to see her favourite teacher, Miss Rigby. Sandra painted pictures of palm trees and zinc-roofed houses in bright bold colours and was transported to a familiar world that made her feel secure and happy.

Some of the new subjects like physics and chemistry still caused her difficulty and she felt she would never catch up as no real help was offered her by the school to make up the lost ground.

One day, well into the term, she was called into the headmaster's office.

'Sandra,' Mr Francis said, 'I have been looking at your reports and it seems that you are having some difficulties.'

Sandra nodded in agreement, hoping that at last she was going to get help.

'I have arranged for you to be tested, and this is Mr Hynson who will conduct the test.'

Sandra glanced nervously in the direction of Mr Hynson, who eyed her through piercing blue eyes over the rims of his spectacles. A well-worn leather briefcase rested on his lap on which he rested both his palms in the proud professional manner that a doctor might display towards his medicine bag.

Sandra wondered what the test was all about, but said nothing as she never questioned those in authority.

'You needn't worry,' Mr Francis reassured her when he saw the anxiety in her eyes. 'It's just a simple test to find out what help you need.'

The headmaster led them to the empty music room where the test was to be conducted, before taking his leave.

Sandra was seated and given a pen and several sheets of printed paper.

'These are to test your verbal, numerical and visio-spatial awareness,' Mr Hynson told her.

Sandra looked at him blankly.

'Don't be put off by the big words,' he added. 'All it means is that you will be tested to check your knowledge of words, numbers and how quick your eye is.'

Sandra reached into her pocket for her handkerchief and wiped the palms of her hands which felt damp and clammy. She wasn't sure why, but she kept her hands under the table so that he wouldn't see her wipe them. She furtively slipped the handkerchief in her pocket, ignoring the beads of perspiration which she felt forming on her forehead.

She told herself that she shouldn't be nervous and that the test was going to be easy. She knew her spelling was quite good, and a lot better than most of the children in her class, and that she wasn't bad at maths, and there wasn't anything wrong with her eyesight.

Mr Hynson paced quietly up and down the room as Sandra glanced over the paper.

The first question seemed straightforward enough – what word completes the first word and begins the second: PRACT (. . .) BERG. She wrote the answer: ICE.

The second question wasn't difficult – there were squiggly

117

shapes set out in two groups of three and each had a circle, a triangle or a rectangle placed at the top. The third set had a rectangle missing which she could see at a glance.

Her confidence rose when she could quickly figure out the answers to later questions. Then she came across a strange one - insert the missing number: 214 (13) 132, 141 ( ) 213.

She had never seen a question like this so she skipped it and came to the next – find the odd man out: ERIC GERANO RUBETT HIRAC.

Sandra was mystified. Perhaps these were old English words that she had yet to learn. What were they getting at? Was it really a test or some kind of joke? Panic set in. She was sweating. She felt the tears swelling in her eyes and wondered if her whole body was going to turn to water.

If only she could think. Maybe the questions weren't so hard after all. If only she knew what they were about. She wished she had known she was going to take the test, so she could have practised.

What if she failed? Would they keep her down in 2C for another whole year? Would everybody call her a dunce? What would Granny think? Oh, Granny, help, help, help.

She cupped her face in her hands and blotted out the test paper in front of her. But she couldn't blot out the sound of the measured footsteps of the examiner pacing to and fro. To Sandra they sounded like the cocky, superior steps of someone who knew all the answers to the test and whose whole existence depended on her not knowing them. She hated him, this heartless stranger who had suddenly turned her world upside down. She opened her eyes and pushed the papers away from her, determined not to finish the rest of the paper.

Mr Hynson, seeing that she was no longer writing, stopped the aimless pacing and came over to her desk. 'Finished then are you?' Sandra resented his chummy, friendly tone, as if he was taking some pleasure in her discomfort.

She nodded. He collected the paper and Sandra dashed out of the classroom before he could say anything. For the rest of the day she sat glumly in class, resolutely keeping her thoughts to herself, and not asking or answering any questions.

As the term wore on she increasingly sought and found refuge in silence. She knew it was illogical, but in class she felt some strange power in her private silent world even if she knew that increasingly the teachers were beginning to think of her as dull and stupid. Let them think what they want, she thought to herself, what do I care?

At school, only Elaine and Miss Rigby had the power to breach the walls she had built up around herself.

A few weeks before half-term she was summoned to the headmaster's study. His eyes were cold and unsmiling.

'I'm afraid you didn't do very well in the test you took. The educational psychologist has recommended that you need special help to bring you up to scratch for you to benefit from a normal school such as ours. I'm afraid I'll be writing to your parents to inform them that you may have to be moved to a special ESN school.'

20 'I wish you left me in Jamaica...'

'ESN school?'

'That's what he said, Mum.'

'What the hell does that mean?' shouted Dad.

'I can't believe that you come all the way from Jamaica to England to end up in a ESN school,' interrupted Mum, all her anger directed at Sandra.

'It's not my fault!' Sandra shot back, surprised at the venom in her voice.

'How you mean is not your fault. Don't is you take the test?'

'I never take an IQ test before and it was strange to me.'

'You must have been wasting your time at school for them to want to send you to a stupid ESN school!'

'What the hell is this ESN school business all about?' asked Dad again.

'E.S.N.' said her mother, dragging out the letters to give them emphasis. 'It mean educationally sub-normal. That's what it mean!'

'What!' he said in disbelief. 'Educationally subnormal? What the hell they trying to say.'

'They trying to say that Sandra too dunce to go to a normal school.'

'Well, I think they off their blasted rocker.'

Sandra was glad that her dad had come to her defence. Putting the school in the dock seemed to take the edge off her mother's anger.

'Sandra,' she said, more in sorrow than in anger, 'you will just have to pull your socks up and settle down with your schoolwork.'

'It's not me you should be talking to,' said Sandra, taking courage from her father's words, 'it's the school you should be talking to.'

'You see,' retorted her mother, 'the workman always blaming his tools.'

'You really think schools in England like schools in Jamaica,' said Sandra with feeling. 'You should go down to the school and have it out with them rather than blame me.'

'Don't speak to me in that tone of voice. You are my daughter and I won't have you bring any of that rudeness to me, you hear!'

But Sandra was too far down the road of defiance to turn back. 'I been telling you and Dadda all along that things not right in that school and all you can say is just ignore them and get on with your work . . .'

'And if you did take our advice you wouldn't come to this.'

'The test was unfair! You still don't believe, do you?' said Sandra, outraged.

'Why would they set you a test that unfair?'

'Granny would believe me if I told her! Granny is my real mother not you!'

Her mother instinctively raised her hands as if to slap her. Then she paused, stung by the full implication of the words. 'So I is not your real mother eh? Is not me, is your grandmother? Eh? Answer me, is your grandmother?'

'I didn't ask you to bring me into this world. I wish you never did.' The tears were now streaming down her face.

Her mother continued undaunted. 'Is your grandmother work her fingers to the bones in that damn hospital washing white people sores and clearing shitty bedpan to feed and clothe you? Is your grandmother scrimp and save and sacrifice to bring you to this country?'

'I wish you left me in Jamaica . . .'

'No, I is not your real mother. All these years I just play-acting. Just putting on a show so people can say I is a good mother.' She went over to the chair at the table and sat down and rested her head in her hands, her face moist with tears.

Sandra regretted her hasty words.

121

'I'm just a failure as a mother. I am just a failure . . .' She started to sob uncontrollably. 'Just a failure . . .'

Sandra's instinct was to console her, but she held back. All her mother could think about was herself and her feelings.

'I hate you,' Sandra sobbed. 'I hate you and I hate England and I hate everybody.' She ran to her room and picked up the folder in which she kept her writing things, dashed over to the coat hanger and putting on her coat went out of the front door slamming it behind her.

Sandra consoled herself that at least there was somebody she could talk to, if only by letter, as she sat down on the cold park bench and began to write to Granny. She had often written to Granny before on the very same bench while the twins played on the swings and slides.

My dearest Granny,
    I am really in big trouble. I am in big trouble at home and at school. They want to send me to another school because they don't think that I can do the work when I know that I can, but it's only that the test they gave me was very strange to me and I am sure I would have a better chance if I got some coaching before the test. Mamma thinks it's my fault because I have been wasting my time at school but that is not true. Also she forget that I spend a lot of time looking after the twins and cooking and looking after the house and can't always do my schoolwork. Granny, I really hate this country.

Sandra paused and looked around the park. It was a sunny day but the crispness in the air owed more to winter than spring. She wished that she had worn her gloves because her hands were cold and stiff, but she persisted with her writing:

I have tried my best to get to like England and to be a good girl like you asked me to but I don't think I could ever feel at home in this country. Granny, there is something that I want to tell you that I never told you before, Mamma and Dadda are not the same as you remember them in Jamaica.

They are different now and I don't think they love me any more. I think they were away from me for too long and now they forget that I am their daughter too. Sometimes I want to run away from home and run away from England. As soon as I grow up and have my own money I will come back to Jamaica and we can live together again.

I am sorry that there aren't any nice things in this letter. I hope that you and Leroy are fine. Bye for now.

    Love,
      Sandra.

As soon as Sandra had finished writing the letter she felt better. Rather than return home, she walked around the park for a while to kill time. Lone elderly people sat on the scattered park benches or strolled leisurely about on their own or in forlorn couples. The trees, the shrubbery and the manicured lawns made Sandra feel that she was in the grounds of a sanatorium rather than a park. In the end she had to leave, it was so depressing.

When she got back home her mother was in the front room on her own. Her father had taken the twins out to the park. He must have guessed that's where she had gone and was probably looking for her. She went into the kitchen to make herself a cup of tea. No sooner had she put the kettle on than she sensed the figure of her mother standing in the doorway.

'Sandra, I want to talk to you.'

Sandra said nothing, but braced herself.

'About what you said . . .'

'I didn't mean what I said, Mamma. I'm sorry.'

'Sandra, you don't understand what we been through in this country. You know what your father and I been through to bring our family back together?'

She spoke softly without any hint of reproach in her voice.

'You think it was easy to get a place to rent, even this dingy little place we call a home? You think it easy to go traipsing from door to door and to see signs saying 'no dogs, no coloured people'? You think I would be cleaning up shit in that hospital

123

today if I had any choice in the matter? You think your father not capable of a better job than working in that factory?'

Sandra felt mortified. Her tears, which had started as a slow trickle, flooded down.

'I'm not saying these things to make you feel bad, Sandra, but you said some hurtful things just now . . .'

'I'm sorry, Mamma, I . . .'

'I know you didn't mean it, Sandra, but sometimes the truth can come out in strange ways. I know I've been too busy with the twins to pay you much mind and be a proper mother to you.'

She reached out and put her arms around Sandra. Sandra let her head rest on her mother's shoulder. Then before they knew it, they were clinging together, the way Sandra had imagined it would have been when they met at the dock in Southampton. And the sobbing started anew.

'Mamma, Mamma,' said Sandra.

When the tears had subsided and the bad feelings between them had dissolved, they stood clinging together silently for a long time, and the spell was only broken by the sound of her father's key in the door.

He read the situation correctly and knew immediately that together they had crossed a turbulent river, and left them alone, taking the twins through to the front room.

Later on, when he judged the time to be right, he said, 'Come, Sandra, sit down, I want to hear about this test.'

Sandra was glad for the opening. She felt they were on her side and it gave her strength. She had stared for so long and hard at the questions that some of them were imprinted on her mind. She fetched pen and paper and wrote down a few of the ones she remembered.

Her father and mother studied the questions for a while. 'And nobody showed you how to do these questions before?' probed her mother.

'Never,' said Sandra emphatically.

'Imagine a thing like that!' Her mother's outrage was genuine.

Turning to her husband she asked, 'You can get Monday morning off?'

'Why you ask?'

'Because I want you to come with me first thing on Monday morning to that school. We are going to have a chat with that headmaster.'

She went into the passage and put on her coat. 'In the meanwhile I have some work to do.'

'Where you going?' queried her dad as she headed downstairs.

But before he got the words out of his mouth, she was gone. He shrugged his shoulders and retired to the sanctity of his bedroom.

Once alone, Sandra got hold of the letter she had written to Granny. She tore it to bits and threw it in the bin. She then sat down and wrote Granny a very different letter.

Sandra didn't have to wait very long for Granny's reply which came just as the second half of the term started again.

Mr Dearest Sandra,

Since your uncle Bertie marry, I have plan to write to tell you we had a real big shot morning wedding, fourteen cars and Mr Smith at the organ. Uncle Bertie dress up sharp as a razor and the bride look real beautiful in her long white dress and veil. It would make all your hearts glad in England if you had seen how much your Granny was admired in my pretty new dress Miss Mack sewed for me and shoes to match. The house was crowded out and we had a juke box and danced till two in the morning when the bride and groom left for Kingston where they are going to live because your Uncle Bertie get a job with the Telephone company paying him eighteen dollars per week. Everybody had a good time and Mrs Simpson was there and Parson too and some of the teachers and a lot of other people many you don't know. Leroy is well but he is still looking when he see a ship at sea or a plane flies low thinking when he will see you again. I am glad to hear that things are better for you in England and I hope that you accustom to the weather by now. My mind was a bit disturb by what you say about the school but I hope that everything will

125

work out for your good for let me tell you now and ever He knows all, let us be thankful for His mercy still endure ever faithful ever sure. In faith believe He is not going to give more hardship than you can bear. Tell your Mamma and Dadda that I have got a woman from the village to come in for half a day in the morning hours to help along with the chores which I know they will be glad to hear. I am old and sick and can only hope that the Father will keep me in the hollow of His hands for except the Lord conduct the plan your best schemes cannot succeed and you labour in vain.

Don't wait so long to write to your Granny again as it make me very happy to get your letters. Love and kisses to Mamma and Dadda and to Wayne and Jean. God bless you and I will keep you all in my prayers.

Love and kisses,
Granny

21 'I am beginning to like England'

The yellow daffodils were the first to announce the arrival of spring, and were eventually joined by a full complement of glorious spring flowers. Until now, daffodils, tulips, and hyacinths were names in books, which gave little indication of the intensity of their colours or the subtlety of their fragrance.

The sense of the earth renewing itself found echoes in the lightness of Sandra's own spirit. She wanted to discard her coat, her cardigan, her shoes and run carefree over the soft mud. But this was England and though the sun shone and nature celebrated, it was still too chilly for such exploits. And, alas, she had no garden of her own in which to run free.

Everybody else's spirit seemed to lift too. The children at school and even the teachers seemed happier and easier to get along with.

And it was thanks to her mum and dad, but mainly to her mum.

On that Saturday morning, over two weeks ago, her mother had travelled halfway across London to visit an old friend of hers from Trinidad, who was a schoolteacher in a secondary school. She had learnt from her all about ESN schools, that they were popularly called 'loony bins' and that many educationalists thought that a lot of children were wrongly placed there, and how difficult it was for any child placed in one ever to get back into a normal school.

Armed with this information, and a fuller knowledge of the IQ test, her mother had gone with her father to the school the following Monday morning and challenged the results of

Sandra's test. The headmaster had been so taken aback he arranged for Sandra to be retested after proper coaching.

Once Sandra had understood that the test was a kind of game and could be fun she was much more confident. This time she passed. Her new-found confidence helped her come to grips with her schoolwork and she began to get better grades all round. Her circle of friends increased too, though Elaine remained her very best friend.

The only cloud that hung over her head was Karen and her gang.

'Let's go to the flicks tomorrow,' proposed Elaine on the last Friday of the term.

There was a general chorus of agreement.

'Are you coming, Sandra?' she asked.

Sandra was too embarrassed to say anything.

'You coming, Sandra?' she repeated.

There was no escape. Sandra had to own up. 'What's the flicks?' She had never heard the term before.

They all burst out laughing. 'The pictures, you dodo!'

'Oh!' said Sandra, comprehending at last and laughing at her own ignorance. 'I'll have to ask my mum.'

Her mum did agree and Sandra found herself rushing to the Underground station early on Saturday afternoon to meet her friends. She arrived breathless to find Elaine, Angela and Barbara, one of the few black girls at the school, and her brother Paul, waiting for her. After the film they went to a hamburger bar and sat around eating and drinking and chatting for ages.

On the way back they noticed the photographic booth in the Underground station.

'Let's take some pictures,' suggested Elaine.

They fed their coins into the machine and, amidst wild shrieks of excitement and delight, scrambled in and out of the booth between flashes to take individual and group photographs.

For the first time since coming to England Sandra saw a happy smiling image of herself. a smile bubbled up from deep inside her and spread itself across her face.

When she got home she sat down and wrote to Granny.

Dearest Granny,

You wouldn't believe it, Granny, but I am beginning to like England a bit more than the last time I wrote to you.

My schoolwork is getting much better and I am beginning to enjoy the lessons. The headmaster said that if I continue to improve I will be able to move up to a better stream next year.

I am enclosing a photo of myself and my best friend Elaine who is at my school. She is the girl I told you about before. We took it in a photographic booth so it isn't very good, but I hope you like it just the same.

Please, Granny, ask Uncle Bertie to send us some wedding pictures. I am really sorry that I missed the wedding especially since I have never been to one before. I really wished that I could have been there to see your dress (smile).

The twins are fine. They want me to tell them stories all the time so I make up stories about Jamaica. I tell them that they have a granny in Jamaica and they are very pleased but they don't fully understand. They say that they want to come to Jamaica to see you. Mamma says that sometimes she wishes they were both girls so that she could dress them up the same, but I think it's nice that they are different. They are now like two chatterboxes and that's partly because they have a grown-up sister around to talk to. On the weekend they always come into my bed in the morning and always end up fighting over the bedcover which ends up on the floor.

Dadda is still working very hard and he says that soon we will be able to buy a house and send for Leroy. I only wish that you could come up too, Granny. If only for a little while.

Me and Mamma are really getting on fine now even if she is very strict about homework and helping around the house.

I think about you and Leroy all the time and I hope that you are now better.

Please, please, Granny, write to me soon.

Lots and lots of love,
   Sandra

Summer brought its own bouquet of surprises for Sandra. Firstly it didn't rain and the sun shone and it was warm and lovely. Most of the time anyway, for there were always days when the weather took a backward step and suddenly it seemed to be winter again with cold grey skies and a constant drizzle. She also discovered to her surprise that the sun stayed out till as late as nine or ten o'clock.

In the afternoons after school, Sandra often took the twins to the park to play in the children's playground. She used to meet up with Elaine and Barbara and Paul and her other new friends.

As the summer term drew to a close and it grew hotter and humid, Sandra found that there was less and less real work being done at school. Everybody was winding down for the summer holidays and Sandra detected a kind of crazed atmosphere in the classroom and playground alike. Tempers flared and cooled again in quick succession. Good friends fought and made up again with amazing regularity. Even Sandra, ever anxious to keep the peace, fell out with Elaine for a few hours over some silly disagreement that they had clean forgotten by the next day.

The one fight that Sandra was dreading came on one of these listless, brooding days. The air was full of the strange smell of rain which reminded her of Jamaica before the onset of the rainy season. She closed her eyes and tried to remember the soothing sound of rainwater on zinc roofs, when suddenly there was a loud clap of thunder and the heavens opened and a deluge of large raindrops clattered noisily against the school roof and concrete pavement.

Sandra and Elaine joined the other children in a wild chase to the one covered area of the playground, where the early arrivals jostled for the few places on the benches. England was so full of surprises, now it had thrown up a tropical-style thunderstorm. The shelter was already crammed with sweaty steaming bodies and the struggle was now for standing space. As Sandra made one

130

last lunge for safety, her path was suddenly blocked by the menacing figure of Karen.

'Ain't no space left,' she scowled.

Sandra backed off and tried to get round behind her, but Karen, like a boxer in a ring, cut off her retreat with a swift sideways step.

'I'm getting wet, let me through,' scowled Sandra in disgust.

'Getting wet, are we?' mimicked Karen. 'You poor, poor thing.'

'Yes, I'm getting wet,' shouted Sandra as the rain started to soak her head and shoulders.

'Well, you can go and shelter somewhere else,' retorted Karen. 'We don't want you here.'

'That's enough,' said Elaine at length.

'Yeah, leave her alone,' said another.

'Knock it off, Karen,' said yet another.

As Karen turned round to confront them, Sandra saw her chance and quickly stepped into shelter. Karen must have had eyes in the back of her head for she swiftly turned round and shoved Sandra back into the rain.

'I thought I told you to keep out?' As she finished her words she reached out again to push Sandra even further away, but Sandra was ready for her and grabbed her by the wrists. Karen made her let go and lunged at Sandra, both hands flailing away with a wild combination of punching and scratching. Sandra grabbed her by the neck with one arm and they fell to the ground. Sandra felt the rainwater against her body. For a moment they tussled for supremacy. Sandra saw the hut as a symbol of England; a place offering shelter from the wind and rain, from which she was being barred. With a desperate heave she wrenched Karen off and in one swift action rolled on top of her. Sandra felt all the anger and frustration of the last nine months pour into her fists, which were now pounding into Karen.

She had little memory of the exact sequence of events after that. All she could remember was being dragged off Karen by some of the other girls, and being led away by Elaine into the toilets where she helped Sandra to dry and compose herself before the afternoon classes started.

The agitation of the fight stayed with her for a few days. Luckily no teachers were around and the incident remained unreported. Sandra would have hated to have blotted her copybook after all the good things that had happened to her at school recently.

Later she came to see the fight with Karen as another murky and treacherous river crossed. She hoped that it was the last river, but what encouraged her more than anything else was the number of children who had been on her side. And there was hope, just a ray of hope perhaps, that her wish might have been granted, for Karen and the rest of her gang avoided her like the plague for the rest of the term.

22 Moving House

Once the summer holidays started Sandra had to look after Wayne and Jean during the day. She couldn't complain about the restriction on her movements for she had nowhere to go, but if ever she felt a bit resentful she consoled herself with the thought that she would have been very lonely on her own at home. She was also glad that she was making some indirect contribution towards the buying of the house because her mum didn't have to pay for a child-minder.

Still, looking after the twins was hard work as she had to prepare their meals and wash their clothes and tidy up after them and keep them from fighting each other or ganging up against her, as well as reading books to them while they cuddled up beside her on the sofa.

Today, Sandra needed a break, so she stuck them in front of the TV to watch a children's programme, and ran a bath. But no sooner had she settled into the bath, than they invaded the bathroom like a couple of marauding pirates.

'Can I come in the bath?'

'Can I come in the bath?'

'No, you can't! Go back and watch the telly, both of you.'

'Please, Sandra?'

'Oh, please, Sandra?'

'No, just leave me alone.'

'I won't be your friend.'

'Me neither.'

'Oh, dear me, I'm so upset.'

'Don't be mean, Sandra.'

'And horrible . . .'

'Wayne, don't even think about taking your shirt off.'

'I mean it. I won't be your friend.'

'Me neither.'

'Jean, put your socks back on.'

'Just for a little while, Sandra.'

'We won't be long. We won't.'

'Jean, take your feet out the bath! The water is too hot for you.'

'It's not too hot!'

'Yes, it is!'

'See, I told you it's not hot for me.'

'Me, neither.'

'Honestly, you two . . .'

'Move up, Sandra.'

'No, you stay down there at the bottom of the bath.'

'It's not fair . . .'

'Not fair!'

'You have the best bit all the time.'

'You take the best part all the time. It's not fair.'

'Well, it's my bath, after all.'

'But it's too hot down here.'

'You want us to burn? You don't care, do you.'

'Listen, I only came here for a peaceful bath.'

'I'll tell Mum.'

'And she will tell you off!'

'Don't be silly, you two.'

'See, it's cooler up here.'

'It's not fair. You let Wayne up there and not me!'

'Please, Jean, don't cry now. OK, OK. You can both stay for five minutes, right!'

'Six minutes.'

'Seven minutes.'

'OK. Seven minutes. Not a second more.'

'Sandra?'

'Yes?'

'Can I get my duck?'

'OK, but don't get the floor wet.'

'Can I get my duck too?'

'Yes, yes, yes . . .'

'And my doll?'

'OK. Wayne, I said not to get the floor wet! Jean, please, there's no space for that boat as well . . .'

Sandra's hopes of a peaceful bath were dashed and, before long, in addition to the twins, she was sharing the bath with ducks and dolls, a yellow plastic boat, and a bucket and spade.

Halfway through the summer holidays she discovered, through a chance encounter with Barbara and Paul in the park, that they lived quite close to her. They were both in England of Trinidadian parents who were fanatical supporters of the Notting Hill Carnival. Every year the entire family had a great time jumping up in the streets of Notting Hill.

'Why don't you come and join the band?' asked Barbara.

'Doing what?'

'I'm going to be in the costume section and Paul is playing in the steel band. The costumes are very nice.'

'Suppose she want to learn to play the steel pan,' interposed Paul.

'And this year the theme is "Land of the Zulus" and I am going to be a Zulu princess,' rejoined Barbara, determined to beat off Paul's challenge.

'It sounds nice,' said Sandra, 'but I have to look after the twins in the days.'

'It's mostly in the evenings and at weekends so that's not a problem. We're going to the mas' camp tomorrow so you can come with us,' said Barbara encouragingly.

'Mas' camp?' queried Sandra.

'Yeah, that's what it's called. That's where we make the costumes and where the band practise,' offered Paul. 'The camp is open every afternoon day except Sundays so we can go any time.'

'Is it far?'

'No, it's only down the Harrow Road. The band is called Eliminators.'

Sandra had never been to a carnival before as the idea of

135

carnival had never caught on in Jamaica. She had no idea what it was all about.

'What do I have to do?'

'You can just help with making the costumes or if you like you can play mas' by being a part of the costume parade.'

'You mean dressing up and marching with the band?'

'Yes, but not marching. Dancing!'

'I have to ask my parents.' The idea of dancing in the streets of London didn't appeal to Sandra, but she figured that she could at least help with making the costumes.

'There are lots of people around so it's safe and the number 18 bus stops outside. We can travel back home together.'

That night she talked it over with her mum and dad after supper.

'This carnival business sound like a waste of time to me,' said Dad.

'Barbara said it was great, Dad. They are playing "Land of the Zulus" this year and it's going to be fantastic.'

He seemed sceptical but in the end he agreed. Sandra met Barbara and Paul early one evening and took the bus to the camp which was situated in the basement of a community centre. Apart from two white men glueing trinkets on to a costume and a white woman who was doing some sewing, all the people were black.

The designs for the various costumes were displayed on the wall above a table. Sandra studied the designs which featured the headdress and costumes used by the Zulus of South Africa. She had never thought much about Africa and what she had seen in films or books was more likely to inspire shame than pride. But the photographs and designs on the wall were an eye-opener for her as she had never guessed at the beauty and magnificence of their dress and beadwork and the stunning beauty of their jewellery.

Sandra and Barbara set to work. They spent ages stringing colourful beads, following the design on the wall, then sewing them together in belt-like strips that were to be worn across the forehead. Then they made beads that would adorn a headdress of

136

green and white and yellow material. Sandra tried one on and the impact was stunning.

The mas' camp was organised along the lines of a factory with an assembly line. While Sandra and Barbara worked on the ornamental headdresses, others worked on the shoulder capes, blankets and aprons that went into the Zulu costumes. All this activity was carried out against a background of loud calypso music belting out from a large transistor on the table.

Although everybody worked hard, there was a lot of time for chatting and making jokes and every now and again people would stop what they were doing and break into dance or song.

When Sandra and Barbara got bored with stringing beads they bought soft drinks and sat round gossiping until it was time to start work again. Sandra felt more at ease than at any other time since leaving Jamaica.

She wondered if she would have the nerve to dance in the streets. From the photographs of last year's carnival on the wall, she realised that she would have to throw off a lot of her inhibitions to enter into the spirit of carnival, Trinidadian-style. But she was determined to put on a costume on carnival day and play mas'. She put her name down for the costume section and promised to pay the necessary ten shillings the next time she came.

A week before the carnival Sandra heard the news. She ran upstairs and pulled out her writing pad and pen.

Dearest Granny,

I have some very good news for you. Dadda and Mamma will be writing to tell you, but I want to be first. We have got a house at last!! Dadda says that all that is needed is for the lawyers to finish the paperwork. He says that he will be looking after Leroy's passage as soon as he and Mamma can find the deposit to pay the travel agent.

I have been to see the house and it is not too far from where we live so it is in the same area. There are three bedrooms and two reception rooms and a kitchen downstairs. Dadda says that one of the rooms downstairs will be turned into a bedroom for Leroy which means that I can have my own room and the twins can have a room to themselves. The house needs a lot of work on it so it will take a while before we can move in. The best part is that there is a nice garden at the back of the house.

Guess what, Granny? I am going to take part in a carnival that will be happening in Notting Hill Gate at the end of this month. There will be lots of costumes and I will be playing mas' with a band that has beautiful Zulu costumes. I will tell you more about it in my next letter.

Granny, if only you came up to England to spend time!! You could always sleep on the sofa in the front room which is quite nice and roomy. I would really love to see you again real soon.

I must rush now, as I have to go off to the carnival camp to help make the costumes. I go there about three times a week during the holidays after Mum gets back from work but I have to get back home by nine o'clock before it starts to get dark.

Please write soon and give my love to Leroy. Everybody sends love.

Your loving granddaughter,
Sandra

They couldn't move till the house was painted and decorated, which would take some weeks, but they started the tedious process of packing their belongings into boxes.

'I never realised we had so much rubbish,' joked Mum.

'I'm gonna throw out half the things I have,' said her dad and he was quite serious though he laughed when he said it. Sandra couldn't remember seeing her parents so happy and it made everybody else in the flat happy too.

In spite of Granny's many entreaties, she had not bothered to pray at all as she had felt so cut off from church and from her own inner spirit, but now every night before she went to bed she knelt down beside her bed and prayed that everything should go well.

Granny didn't take long to reply to her letter.

My dearest Grandchild,

I was glad to hear from you and to learn that our prayers have found an answer in Heaven for when we pray earnestly the Father will never turn a deaf ear to our pleas but will listen knowing all our needs and if things are hard He will make them soft. I speak with Leroy about the house and about his going to England and I tell him that he is going to have a better time of it than you because you already pave the way for him and now that your father have bought a house you will all feel more settled. I receive your father letter a few days after yours and it seem that Leroy will be with you before Christmas if all goes well. Leroy is a constant help to me especially in times of trouble for he goes to the drugstore to fetch my medicine for me and goes to the shops to get the little things I need. I hope that you enjoyed your carnival. We don't have anything like that here in Jamaica only masquerade.

I will miss Leroy when he leave. You know to have a house full of your own children and later your own grandchildren and then you see them go one by one from you and you are left alone, only God can cure the ache that you feel in your heart but I always have a hope that I will see you again some day and also to see your Mamma and Dadda and to see Wayne and Jean for the first time.

Your ever loving Grandmother

Moving house was a very happy event. Unlike her parents' home in Jamaica or Granny's house, Sandra felt no attachment to the flat. The excitement of moving into the new house gave her mother renewed strength and vigour. Her father did most of the packing and was in an unusually buoyant mood most of time. He was off night-shift work and had cut back on his overtime. How long the new state of affairs would last, Sandra didn't dare guess.

Sandra did her share of packing. As she packed away the toys in the bedroom she shared with the twins, she came across Lizzie, lying on the floor, neglected and with one arm still missing. The twins seemed to have lost interest in her as their affections had been transferred to the teddy bears which they had been given for their birthday earlier that summer.

She felt remorse for her neglect as she gathered her up in her arms as if she were a nurse and Lizzie a war victim. Then she found the missing arm and clicked it back into the gaping shoulder socket. She stroked her hair for a minute then gave her one last kiss before placing her in a cardboard box. She closed it and put it with a pile of other boxes which were destined for the attic of the new house.

When the day for moving came and all that was left were the carpets and the usual fixtures and fittings, the flat was empty and sad. This was one river she was glad to cross, and Sandra left without a backward glance as they piled into the van her father had hired for their new home.

Fifteen minutes later they pulled up in front of their new house. Just when they had caught their breath they had to start work again. Up the stairs, down the stairs, then up and down again till every last item was transferred from the van to the house.

Sandra was pleased with her room and when she had unpacked her things and cleaned it she wandered downstairs and into the room that was to be Leroy's. It was one of the reception rooms which had been used as a dining room. They were going to eat in the kitchen.

Leroy was due to be with them for Christmas, three long months away. Such a pity that Leroy won't be here for the carnival, she thought.

23 Carnival

Carnival day arrived and Sandra had persuaded her parents to come and to bring the twins. It took a little while convincing her father that it would be fun.

They took the bus down to the camp where many of the bands were assembling. The sun was shining and there were people parading around in a variety of colourful costumes proclaiming their membership of one band or another. There were simple costumes and elaborate costumes and already the crowds were several thousands strong. Sandra had never seen so many black faces in one place before in England.

There was a wonderfully festive atmosphere. A little distance up the road a steel band was playing a vigorous road-march tune, the sharp metallic notes splitting the air. From the direction of Ladbroke Grove could be heard the deep throbbing bass guitars being pumped out by rival sound systems.

Everywhere people were in high spirits, chatting and drinking and milling about waiting for the carnival to get under way. Groups of policemen were around, some were busy directing traffic and others keeping a wary eye on things.

She spotted Paul on the back of a lorry playing with the steel band.

She darted into the camp, leaving her mum and dad to wait on the pavement, where some of the band, already in costume, milled about. She went to find her costume and ran into Barbara, who was already in hers. She helped Sandra change and then they went over to a mirror on the wall and admired themselves in their Zulu outfits, which were all the more marvellous when seen beside others.

Sandra joined a queue to have her face painted. She watched as peoples' faces were transformed with green and red and blue and black face paint. To top it all, a translucent coat of glitter was added.

At last her turn came. She had never had her face painted before and she began to experience that shift in her perception of reality as she looked at the result in the mirror. She felt as if she was in disguise, that for the day she was going to be somebody else, and that somebody else was one of her very own ancestors.

She followed the rest of the band into the street under a canopy of gaily coloured balloons and they proclaimed their presence by a shrill of the whistles which they each carried around their necks as part of their costumes.

Sandra took her place in the band between the lengths of ropes held by stewards on both sides of the players. The band struck up and amidst another shrill of whistles the procession moved forwards. The dancing started in earnest.

As they moved up the street spectators jostled on every side to take photographs. There was even a film crew. Sandra felt more like dancing than she had ever done before. 'We have the whole day ahead of us,' cautioned Barbara with a smile, 'so make sure you pace yourself.'

Sandra didn't pay her a blind bit of notice. One way or the other she was going to be there dancing at the end of the carnival.

A minibus attached to the band travelled behind the procession. It served as a makeshift rest room and restaurant rolled into one. In addition there were scores of vendors selling a variety of food and drinks with a Caribbean flavour. Most popular were stalls with roasted corn, peppery fried fish, fried chicken, fried plantains and roti with curried mutton or changa. Chilled canned drinks were on sale at virtually every stall. Some vendors sold from makeshift stalls set up at the side of the street or even from the back of vans or cars. There was even a woman with a handcart, from which she sold shaved ice and syrup, just like back home. Dad bought some fried fish and corn for Sandra and Mum, and the twins enjoyed crisps in preference to the cooked food.

Within an hour they were under the bridge next to Ladbroke Grove Station. The overhead motorway trapped the sound and the dancing intensified as the procession slowly shunted past the station and headed towards the Grove and the heart of the carnival where the judges decided which bands should get prizes.

There were prizes for the best designer, the players who best showed off their costumes, the best king and queen, the best small-scale band and the best large-scale band and prizes too for the best individual male and female costumes.

After following the carnival route for what seemed like hours the band arrived for the judging. Costumes were straightened and last-minute repairs carried out, especially to the large costumes of the king and queen.

The whistling grew shriller and the volume of the music swelled as they danced in front of the judges. Sandra lost the last of her inhibitions in a frenzy of dancing. For that moment she was a Zulu princess, proud and exuberant and with no other purpose on her mind than impressing the judges.

She looked round and caught sight of her mum and dad dancing for all they were worth on the fringes of the band. The twins were in their double push-chair, fast asleep. Once the band had passed in front of the judges they relaxed and danced more mechanically for the finale of their carnival had passed. Now that it was over Sandra felt utterly drained.

They made their way back to the camp, slowly walking behind the band. It was now twilight and they wilted visibly, and had to sit on the low wall that ran near the pavement. Their ears were still ringing from day-long exposure to the steel drums. Sandra felt elated. It was as if she had been drained of all the tensions and anxieties that had accumulated in her body during the course of the eventful year. If only Leroy were here, her cup of happiness would overflow.

They eventually went inside the camp and took off their costumes. They then joined the queue in the kitchen and collected paper plates, laden with rice and peas and chicken and salad, before escaping the heat of the kitchen to eat contentedly outside in the cool night air.

They could still hear the distant roar of the carnival in full swing. But it was getting late, so Sandra bid her friends good night, went on the bus with her parents and the twins, and headed for home.

As they walked down their street towards the house, Sandra squeezed between her parents and put her arms around them. It was the first spontaneous gesture of affection she had shown them since she came to England. Nobody said a word as they walked the last few steps to their door arm in arm.

Before Sandra went to bed, she had a long luxuriating soak in a hot bath. Then, sitting up in bed, she wrote to Granny.

Dearest Granny,

Today I had the happiest day of my life in England. I have just come back from the carnival and I spent the whole day dancing through the streets dressed up in a pretty Zulu costume. Granny, you must believe me when I tell you we don't have a carnival in Jamaica and it is difficult to imagine what it is like. I won't know until tomorrow if our band won a prize, but I had such a good time that I don't really care. I persuaded Mamma and Dadda to come and they took the twins. They all enjoyed themselves and can't wait for the next carnival.

I am very excited that Leroy will be coming up soon. There are only three bedrooms upstairs, so Dadda has turned the dining room downstairs into a bedroom for him. I am helping him to put up new wallpaper and to paint the room. The kitchen is big enough for a dining table, so that's where we eat our meals.

The best part is the garden, though it is still a bit overgrown. Mamma has planned where all the new plants will go in spring, though she says that it's Dadda's job to clear it.

Wayne and Jean would love to see you too as I speak about you a lot, and they know so much about you. They remind me all the time that you are their granny too, not just mine.

Mamma and Dadda are fine and send their love. We get along much better now and they are so much nicer to me.

I spoke to Dadda and he promised me that after Leroy comes up, he is going to save up so that you can come and visit us. It would really be nice if you could come when I have my summer holidays, when you won't get cold and I will have lots of time to spend with you.

It's a long while now since I had a letter from you so please write soon.

Lots and lots of love
Sandra

School started again in September and the memory of the carnival faded with time. Sandra's old routine of getting ready for school, helping with the twins, homework then school again, re-established itself.

But things were much better now in the relative comfort of the new home. Mum and Dad found more time to keep an eye on Sandra and to monitor her progress at school. They discovered that there were battles to be fought on Sandra's behalf, when they learnt that she had been placed in the middle or bottom classes in some subjects when they thought she was capable of being in the top classes.

They had more confidence in confronting the headmaster and succeeded in getting Sandra moved up into the top groups in maths and English and in getting Mr Francis to review her other subjects at the end of the year. They had a lot of support from Miss Rigby and some of the other teachers, who had encouraged Sandra.

By the middle of October the leaves on the trees had gradually turned to a golden brown. There was a large horse-chestnut tree at the bottom of their garden which shed its large leaves to form a rusty brown carpet over the lawn.

It was Wayne who first spotted the squirrel from the back window. 'Sandra, look! A squirrel.'

'Where?'

'There.'

Sandra and Jean peered through the window and watched the squirrel as it searched for chestnuts. She was surprised to see a squirrel so far from the park.

'He's got a conker in his hands,' said Jean.

They hurried down to the garden and tried to approach the squirrel. But the little creature scampered away when they got close.

At the insistence of the twins, Sandra ran lengths of string through the conkers that littered the garden. They all had turns at being conker champion before tiring of the game. Then they scattered the leaves with their feet and when they were bored with that, they gathered bundles of leaves in their hands and hurled them at each other.

That Saturday, while her mum was away shopping with the twins, Sandra helped her dad to rake up the leaves and transported wheelbarrow-loads to the compost heap at the bottom of the garden which he had prepared. Already the compost heap gave off the musty smell of rotting vegetables and decayed leaves, bramble and grass cuttings, and rose higher and higher with each new barrow-load of leaves.

Afterwards they tackled the neglected flower-beds which were overgrown with weeds. Sandra felt as if she was walking in quicksand, for soggy clumps of earth clung to the shoes she wore, which were an old pair belonging to her mother.

'It's the clay in the soil that's causing that,' explained her dad. 'There is a lot of clay in the London soil. You can't escape it.'

She enjoyed working in the garden with her father. It stirred childhood memories of Jamaica when she had helped him with his vegetable patch by handing him the grain as he sowed it. Now she was a much more active partner, and side by side they hoed and raked and turned over the dark earth with fork and spade.

'If we don't turn over the soil now, it won't be so fertile in spring,' he explained.

Sandra looked around at the trees which now stood with skeletal dignity against the sky. She could detect buds that were already swelling with the promise of new leaves in spring.

Then they heard the faint ring of the doorbell. They were hardly settled in the house and hadn't received many visitors, so the sound of the bell was still strange to their ears.

'Run and answer the door, Sandra,' he said, and before she

147

reached the kitchen door he shouted after her, 'And don't forget to take those shoes off.'

Sandra kicked off the muddy shoes and ran through the house to the front door and saw a postman with a telegram. She signed for the telegram and went to the kitchen door and called her father.

'It's a telegram for you, Dad.'

Her father rushed across the damp muddy lawn and tore open the telegram and read it and then slumped down on the concrete kitchen steps.

'What is it, Dad?' Sandra asked, but he sat in silence with bowed head, the telegram crumpled in his hands.

At length he got up and removed his shoes before coming inside.

'What's wrong, Dad?' Sandra was unable to bear the suspense.

He looked at her as if contemplating whether to tell her or not. Then he put his hand on her shoulder and led her to the front room. 'Sit down, Sandra, I have some sad news.' He had to look at the telegram again.

'Yes, Dad?' she prompted with mounting anxiety.

'It's Granny,' he said. 'Granny died yesterday. She died of kidney failure.'

Sandra tried to say something but no words escaped her lips. She raised her hands to her face. She could hardly breathe.

'Granny dead, Granny dead,' she said at last. She could not fight back the tears. She ran up to her room and threw herself on the bed and sobbed bitterly. Her tears could not relieve the arc of pain around her heart. She could only think of one way to ease the pain. She got up from the bed and went over to her desk and took out her writing pad and pen.

My dearest Granny,

Why did you have to go and die before I could see you again? There are so many things that I wanted to say to you that I could not say in a letter. Most of all, Granny, I wanted to tell you that I loved you. I tried many times to write it in my letters to you but the words would not come

148

because I was too shy. Now I wish that I had been brave enough to say those words. Wherever you are I hope that you can hear me now. I always called you Granny, but you were also my mother and my father and I will never forget the kind words of advice you gave me. You always prayed for me even when I forgot how to pray for myself and you always believed that things would turn out all right in the end when things looked so gloomy to me. You were the best granny anyone could ever wish to have because you always listened to me and heard what I had to say and I want to thank you for that.

I am glad that I painted your picture which I will always keep to remind me of you.

This is one letter that I will never post but wherever you are, Granny, I hope you will hear me when I say that I love you and I hope that you will rest in peace.

Goodbye, Granny.

From your ever loving granddaughter,

Sandra

25 Flowers for Granny

Sandra tried her best to explain to Wayne and Jean: 'Granny has gone away to a resting place.'

'When is she coming back?'

'She won't be coming back.'

'Why won't she be coming back?'

'Because she is tired and she is very happy there.'

'Can we go to see her?' asked Jean.

'Yes,' intervened Mum. 'One day we will all go to Jamaica on a nice holiday and we can see all our relatives and visit Granny at her resting place.'

'We are going to go to Jamaica, we are going to go to Jamaica,' shrieked the twins in delight.

'Sandra, are you coming to Jamaica with us?'

'Yes, I'll come to Jamaica with you and we can take some flowers for Granny.'

'Are we going after we go to sleep and wake up?'

'No, not tomorrow,' said Sandra.

'After we go to sleep and wake up and go to sleep and wake up again?'

Sandra laughed and tried her best to explain that it would be quite a long while before they could go. Years maybe. Then she gave them both a big hug.

Back in Jamaica, Leroy and the extended family of aunts and uncles had taken charge of the funeral arrangements which were relayed to London in a series of telegrams.

Dad wanted to attend the funeral but the expenses of buying the house and moving and paying for Leroy's passage to England had exhausted whatever savings they had and the mortgage repayments were onerous. His only chance lay with the horses, and he spent an entire day in the betting shop, but came home despondent and crestfallen.

On the day of the funeral he broke down and cried like a child. He wept for his dead mother but even more he wept because he couldn't be there at her funeral to pay his last respects; because he couldn't be there to celebrate the Nine Nights afterwards, to sing and dance and make merry to help her spirit on its last homeward journey. But Leroy was there. Sandra thought of him, alone and bearing the burden of all their grief, and felt sorry for him.

The only good thing that came from Granny's untimely death was that the date for Leroy's departure for England had to be brought forward. He was coming to England a whole month earlier than had been planned. He was coming by air, for though it was more expensive than by sea, everybody thought that, in the circumstances, he should be with his family as soon as possible.

The day arrived and they all went to Paddington Station by bus and took a coach to Heathrow Airport. After an anxious wait, the arrival of his plane was announced. They made their way down to the arrivals lounge to meet Leroy.

Sandra remembered her arrival at Southampton, and wondered if Leroy would be experiencing the same emotions she had felt at the time. She peeled her eyes for the first sight of Leroy. She didn't have long to wait. He came into view carrying an Air Jamaica shoulder-bag and pushing a large trolley bearing his suitcases. She couldn't get over how much he had grown in one year.

'Leroy, Leroy!' Sandra shouted. She broke away from her little family group and ran down the passage to Leroy and flung her arms around him. Leroy smiled and hugged her in return.

The ice was broken. Her parents, as if to make up for the awkwardness of the time they had met Sandra, hugged him warmly. The twins hid behind their mother's legs and giggled.

Dad took Leroy's shoulder-bag and took charge of the suitcases and marshalled them towards the coach. He had the air of a mother hen who was gathering up the last of her chicks under his wings.

After routine questions about the flight were out of the way, and they had boarded the coach, Dad asked about the funeral.

'It was a very good funeral,' answered Leroy.

'A lot of people came?'

'People came from all over. Even from Westmorland and Manchester.'

'That's good.'

'There were a whole heap of cars there. I never know Granny knew so many people.'

'Sixty-eight years is a long time,' said Dad.

'How did the Nine Nights go?' asked Mum.

'Uncle Bertie and Aunt Madge look after that. They could only stay for four days as Uncle Bertie couldn't get more time off work. But a lot of people help out for the rest of the Wake.'

'She lived a hard life, but she at rest now,' said Mum, reaching across and holding Leroy's hand.

Dad placed his hands on top of hers. 'What is important is that we are all together again.'

Sandra choked back the tears. From what she saw and heard, she realised that her parents too had crossed many rivers of their own.

'Is she nice?' she asked Leroy.

'Who?' asked Leroy.

'Aunt Madge, of course!'

Leroy smiled. 'Yes, she is very nice. I brought some wedding photos.' He opened his shoulder-bag and took out the photos.

'She's very pretty,' said Mum.

'Lucky man,' said Dad.

'Let me see,' said Wayne.

'Let me see,' said Jean.

As they poured over the photographs, Leroy took a small box from the bag. He opened it and handed Sandra a brown envelope. 'Granny left this for you.'

Sandra held the envelope for a while, trying to guess what was inside. At length she tore open the envelope. It was Granny's gold wedding band attached to a crucifix pendant.

'Thank you, Granny,' she said softly to herself, slipping the chain around her neck and fondling the ring. She knew that it hadn't left Granny's finger for over forty years and was of great sentimental value to her.

'She gave me this,' said Leroy, showing her an old watch and chain which used to belong to their grandfather.

'We haven't got a present,' said Jean.

'That's not fair,' said Wayne.

Leroy looked at Sandra and smiled. 'Granny had this specially made for you, Jean.' He handed her a gold bangle which had her name engraved on the inside. Granny's present for Wayne was a bracelet with his name also engraved on the nameplate.

Sandra was moved that Granny must have spent the last of her savings on the presents. But she had no time to dwell on the matter, for there were lots of questions she had for Leroy and lots of interesting landmarks she had to point out on the journey home.

A few days later, after Leroy had rested and fully recovered from jet lag, Sandra decided to take him to meet some of her friends. It was a cold day. Leroy shivered and his teeth chattered.

Sandra laughed. 'You'll soon get accustomed to it,' she assured him.

As they were headed down the street they came to a church whose doors were open.

'I have an idea,' said Sandra. She beckoned Leroy and they mounted the steps and entered the church.

It was empty and had a quiet and serene atmosphere. It was the first time she had been inside a church since Christmas. An elderly black woman was arranging a display of flowers on the altar. She flashed them a smile.

At the rear of the church there was a smaller altar with rows of candles. A few were lit. Sandra bought a candle and lit it and placed it with the others, then took a candle and gave it to Leroy, who did the same. Then she said a short prayer for Granny.

When they left the church it was snowing.

'Leroy, look! Snow! Snow!'

Leroy couldn't understand what all the fuss was about.

'Is this first time you are seeing snow?' he teased.

'Yes,' she said. 'The very first time.'

They bent down and picked up some snow from the ground.

'So this is what it's like,' said Sandra. She tasted it. 'It melts in your mouth, just like candy floss.'

They walked in the gently falling snow to the park. Elaine, Barbara and Paul were waiting for them. Sandra hardly had time to introduce Leroy to her friends before a fierce snowball fight broke out.

They threw snowballs in all directions. Sandra got more ambitious as the fight raged and made bigger and bigger snowballs which she aimed with deadly accuracy. She found herself laughing more than she had in all of her time in England.

As she walked home with Leroy and her friends, Sandra was overcome by a feeling of well-being. She didn't know for sure what the future in England held for her, but she knew that there would be many more rivers to cross. She would remember Granny's words, that to get across you sometimes have to lighten your load and she knew that resentment, hate, fear and even grief had to be offloaded.

Sandra was sure that, however deep the rivers, or however turbulent their waters, she would get across to the other side.